SANDRA BUNINO

EVERNIGHT PUBLISHING ®

www.evernightpublishing.com

PLATINUM

Copyright© 2018

Sandra Bunino

Editor: Karyn White

Cover Artist: Jay Aheer

ISBN: 978-1-77339-776-4

SANDRA BUNINO

DEDICATION

To Leisha, Mr. M, and Weezy

SANDRA BUNINO

PLATINUM

Platinum, 1

Sandra Bunino

Copyright © 2018

Chapter One

The electronic song of slot machines provided the backdrop for the replay of the past twenty-four hours of Stacia Howell's life. She regretted ignoring the warning sirens blasting in her head when she boarded the Vegas-bound plane. Her father had always told her it was the devil's playground. She hated when he was right. Only a day ago, she'd been lured to Las Vegas with the promise of a hot tip that would've skyrocketed her career. Today, at what the hell time is it anyway, she sat in a booth at an all-you-can-eat buffet that stank of hotdogs, stale cigarette smoke, and B.O. with only a few crumpled dollars in her pocket. She'd left everything else in the hotel room she'd fled less than an hour ago.

She tapped her fingernails on the smudged glass of iced tea the waitress had practically dropped on the table and blew a long breath from pursed lips as she scanned the nearly empty restaurant. One other booth was occupied by an older couple busy flipping through a tour pamphlet. She poked at the ice cubes with the straw and took a sip, hoping it would calm her nerves and give her an idea of what to do next. Without money, credit cards, ID, and cell phone, her options were severely limited. She'd have to nurse the free iced tea for another hour while her credit card company approved her identity and allowed her to charge a plane ticket. She'd rather wait it out than call her boss for help, or worse, her father. He'd haul her ass to Cleveland faster than a Roulette wheel spin. She glanced at her watch as a shadow blanketed the table.

"Get up, Princess. You're coming with me." A deep voice rumbled from above.

A wall of black blocked her exit from the booth. Her eyes trailed up the back of a leather jacket, lingered on a set of football player shoulders, and finally to a shock of dark, cropped hair.

"Won't tell you again. Get up," he grumbled.

Following a stranger had caused her to end up in her present predicament, and she wasn't about to make it worse by doing it again. "Did Jake send you?" She blinked back tears as the severity of her situation took hold.

"No one sends me anywhere, Princess."

Before she could react, his hand encircled her wrist.

"What the..." She pulled back, but he had the grip of a cobra. Her eyes tipped to a barbed wire tattoo peeking from under his sleeve. He gave her arm a tug, pulling her like a ragdoll as he dragged her to her feet.

"Let go of me or I'll scream," she said between clenched teeth.

"I wouldn't do that unless you want your pretty head blown off," said the same steady and calm voice.

She gulped. Her eyes darted to the man who had a vise grip on her arm. Dark stubble covered his chiseled features, and a pair of sunglasses completed his up to no good look. "Hey, Man in Black wannabe, I'm not playing your game. If you don't let go of me now I'll sure as hell scream." He scared the shit out of her, but she had enough sense to remember at least one of the rules she'd learned while reporting on a self-defense segment: stay in a public place and make as much noise as possible.

"See that guy?" Her eyes flicked in the direction of his nod. A monster of a man in a t-shirt with tree trunk sized tattooed biceps glared back. "Jake's bosses sent him. His orders are to escort you to the dumpsters behind the kitchen as soon as you walk out of here."

She was caught in the middle of a nineteen-seventies mobster movie. But the man glaring at her was as real as the sweat forming on her brow. She tried to swallow again; however, the lump taking residence in the back of her throat prevented the action. "And do what?" Her voice was barely a whisper.

"What you do you think?" He loosened his grip on her wrist and slid his palm up to capture her forearm.

"If that's true, what's going to stop him?"

"Me." His right hand snaked around her waist, and he pulled her against his side. "Eyes down and walk with me."

"Why should I listen to you?" Her gaze bounced from one thug to the other, and his grip tightened.

"It's him or me. Take your pick."

She glanced around for support, but the restaurant was suddenly empty. The waitress was nowhere in sight, and the old couple had vanished. Her gaze searched the empty hostess stand as he led her toward the exit and closer to the wall of muscle standing a few feet away.

She kept her eyes tracked to the floor as her pointed toe pumps stepped in unison with the pair of black leather boots of her captor. However, she'd only heard the clicking of her shoes as he guided her down a marble flooded hallway. His footfalls were silent. Her feet were killing her. "Where are we going?"

"This way." He stopped at a door and threw a glance over his shoulder before letting go of her forearm and fishing a card from his pocket which he slid through a black box on the wall. A soft buzz sounded. He pulled the door open and tugged her inside.

"That didn't answer my question," she said, slowing down her pace.

"Keep moving, Princess. You're not safe yet." The heat of his hand at the small of her back seared her exposed skin as her shirt hitched from the waistband of her pants.

She stumbled, and her heel snapped. "Wait. My shoe." She stopped and held his shoulder for balance as she pulled off her pump and hobbled a few steps with one good shoe.

"You're slowing us down," he growled. With a hand planted on her back, he scooped her into his arms in one fluid movement. They zigzagged through a series of corridors until he stopped at a door with a small, square window. He stepped back, kicked the horizontal bar, and a whoosh of warm air hit her cheeks.

She blinked as he carried her into the darkness, and panic zipped through her body. She kicked frantically, trying to free herself from his grip. "Where are you taking me?" She hardly recognized her shaky voice.

His grip tightened around her at the unanswered question. The purr of a motor filled her ears as her vision adjusted to the inky night and Stacia's eyes settled on a man, standing next to a black SUV, who nodded as he opened the back door where she was dropped inside.

"Move over." Her captor climbed in next to her, and the other man got behind the wheel. They sped off so fast her body slammed into the door. "Better put your seatbelt on," he said without a glance in her direction.

She did as he said and tilted her face to get a look at her kidnapper. "Tell me where you're taking me," she repeated.

"You don't need to know right now."

"Yes, I do!" Her shrill voice even hurt her own ears.

"The way I see it, you're not in the position to make demands, and if you continue screaming we'll drop you in the desert. If Jake doesn't find you, I'm sure you'll make a hungry coyote's day."

Stacia opened her mouth to argue, but the image of a mangy coyote dropped in her head and she snapped it closed. She scanned her surroundings. Bright lights from the street cast colorful designs along the leather interior. But after a few minutes the lights were few and far between. She knew enough about Vegas to know they'd left the city. Nothing but a few houses dotting the dark desert landscape lay outside the car.

"Anyone following us, Benjamin?"

"No, sir. Haven't seen a set of headlights behind us in at least ten miles. Radar isn't picking up anything in the air either."

He nodded, and his shoulders softened. He pulled his glasses off and rubbed his eyes.

Radar? What would follow them in the air? She turned to him and set her shoulders. "I need to know what's going on. Who the hell are you? And where are we going?"

He met her stare. His ocean blue eyes took her by surprise. They were like a bright beacon in a turbulent sea. However, there was no warmth in his gorgeous eyes as his gaze unapologetically washed over her body and tipped back to her face. "Name's Walker."

Her heart took its place back in her chest. Somehow knowing his name slightly calmed her nerves. "That's a start. Is Walker your first or last name?"

"It's the only one you need to concern yourself with."

She kept his gaze. "Fine. What about my next question?"

"I told you, you don't need to know that right now."

Stacia narrowed her eyes. "Are you going to kill me?"

The corner of his mouth quirked. "No, Princess. I don't plan to kill you, and I'm going to make sure no one else does either."

She let out a breath she didn't realize she held. "It's Stacia. My name's Stacia."

"I know who you are."

She narrowed her eyes. "What else do you know about me."

"Your name is Stacia Howell. Reporter for KCLA."

Name and occupation. That information could be easily found with a few clicks online.

"I also know you live in LA. You're twenty-six and single. You have an online dating profile but haven't swiped right on anyone. You don't have any strong personal ties in LA or anywhere else. Your father is a retired general with the United States Army, and he's the only family you have."

"Who the fuck are you?" she asked, throwing shade in his direction.

His gaze never strayed from the windshield, but his neck worked a hard swallow. "The guy who saved your life," he said evenly.

Stacia faced her reflection in the window. The white highway line streaked by as his words sank in. He may have saved her from being shot and left to die in a grungy dumpster, but she was still being held against her will. He had control; she had none. She needed to find a way to change that. She squinted into the black night. Even if the landscape held a hint of where they were headed, she'd never be able to see it since the route was devoid of streetlights. She was out of options, and she was obviously not going to be provided any information soon. She rubbed her eyes and leaned her head into the soft leather. Her thoughts scattered, but exhaustion settled over her eyes. She'd only close them for a few moments…

Chapter Two

"Wake up, Princess."

The huskily spoken words trickled into her brain, rousing her from a crazy dream. But it didn't take her long to remember the events over the past day weren't a dream at all and the voice slipping through her veins and making her toes curl was very real. Car doors opened and slammed as she blinked the sleep from her eyes. Her door swung open, and the hazy light of dawn greeted her as Walker's fingers wrapped around her forearm.

"Are you always so flippin' grabby?" she muttered as she almost fell out of the SUV and the balls of her feet fell upon sharp gravel. She hopped back onto the seat. "I can't walk on that." She rubbed her foot.

"Come on." He pulled her to the outside step of the SUV and lifted her up like he had at the casino.

"You don't have to carry me. Let me get my shoes." Stumbling around on a broken heel would've been less embarrassing than being carried around like some damsel in distress. Her request was met with silence. She continued her protest until her eyes followed the long strip of gravel. A metal hangar stood at one side and a couple single propeller planes that almost blended in with the sandy desert floor were parked outside. She squinted at the emblem on the side of one of the small aircrafts to figure out her location: US Air Force. "You're in the military?" A calm melted over her body.

"Not exactly," he answered flatly.

So much for her momentary ease. Her mind raced to form a plausible connection as he carried her toward the back of the SUV where a gleaming white jet sat waiting. She shook her head. "I'm not going in there."

"It's not up for discussion," he said, heading for the set of stairs leading to the opening of the plane. As they ascended the staircase she recognized the print near the door. Her heart kicked in her chest as she read the word "Platinum" printed in stylized script. Walker unceremoniously dropped her on her feet at the top of the staircase and waved his hand as she stepped inside. Her gaze moved through the interior decorated in muted shades of silver and blue. Instead of rows of seats that were standard on commercial planes, the cabin consisted of four reclining chairs at each window and a small bar with a recessed screen on the wall.

Stacia spotted a door at the back of the cabin. "Bathroom?" she asked, hoping for a few minutes to collect her thoughts and make sense of the clusterfuck that was suddenly her life.

Walker nodded from his spot at the jet's entrance. She was relieved to put some distance between herself and Walker, and Stacia's feet sank into the plush carpet as she stepped to the bathroom and yanked the door open. The room was illuminated in soft light, which was the only similarity to the minuscule plane restrooms she was used to. Instead of a two-by-two-foot lavatory compartment, this one looked like it belonged in a luxury hotel suite with gleaming fixtures and marble countertop. It was bigger than her own bathroom. Shit, it was almost bigger than her whole apartment. Stacia's gaze hit the mirror. Mascara tracked down her cheeks, her hair stuck up in different directions, and her linen pants resembled a crumpled napkin. She splashed cold water on her face and patted it dry with a fluffy towel. Placing her palms on the cool counter, she stared at her reflection and retraced the steps that brought her to the powder room of a private jet. It started with a story that would've blown the roof off her career. Her so-called informant, Jake, wouldn't give her much information up front. The only thing he said was Platinum Enterprises and its elusive owner were smack in the middle of it. The fact that she was on Platinum's jet wasn't all that bad. If she played her cards right, she could return with an even better story, if she didn't get herself killed first.

She ran her fingers through her knotted hair before facing the man who now controlled her future. Her ears perked at the sound of male voices as she opened the door. She recognized Walker's slow and even tone. At least her body did. It did funny things to her insides. His low grumble sailed through her and nestled low in her belly. Even though his voice didn't contain an ounce of warmth, it had her hot, bothered, and wondering how it would sound against her ear, in the dark, as he did all sorts of dirty things to her.

Her cheeks flushed, and she shook her head. *What the hell?* She should've been more concerned with getting out of her present situation, not jumping into the sack with Walker the Bounty Hunter or whoever he thought he was.

The two men stopped talking when she opened the door. Her eyes locked on Walker. His stony features were still except for a slight flinch of his cheek as his gaze moved from her to the guy standing next to him holding a shopping bag. Walker narrowed his eyes, pulled his phone from his pocket, and strode to the platform outside the plane.

The man she recognized as the driver, Benjamin, worked up a polite smile and approached her with his right arm outstretched. "We haven't properly met. I'm Benjamin, Walker's assistant."

She met his handshake. "Stacia." *Duh.* "But you already knew that." She tilted her head to get a better view over Benjamin's shoulder. "What's wrong with him?"

Benjamin shifted slightly, blocking her view.

"Nothing at all. Walker asked me to pick you up a few things to make you comfortable for the flight. I hope everything is to your liking." He handed her the shopping bag.

She held it open and peered at the bundles neatly wrapped in tissue paper and a designer shoe box. "You just picked me up a few things as we raced through the desert in the middle of the night." She eyed him suspiciously. "Where'd it come from?"

His smile didn't break. "We'll be taking off soon. You can take that seat after you're changed." Benjamin pointed to the front seat opposite the door, turned and strode to Walker, leaving Stacia no other option than to do as he requested.

She returned to the bathroom and emptied the contents of the bag onto the counter. A small bag of toiletries and cosmetics were included with a bra, panties, a pair of jeans, a white silk blouse, and a pair of soft leather flats. She checked the tags of each item to find everything was her size. Stacia changed, brushed the knots from her hair, and tied it back in a loose bun before washing her face and brushing her teeth. She swiped a coat of gloss on her lips, and her mood brightened slightly. She was almost convinced they weren't going to kill her. Why would they go through the trouble to buy her expensive clothes if they were going to push her out of the plane? What a waste of a great blouse. She shoved her old clothes into the bag, opened the door, and her heart jumped to her throat. Walker stood in the doorway, his eyes blazing down at her. "Jeez. Lurk much?"

His gaze washed over her and lingered at her chest. She looked down and noticed she'd missed a button and her cleavage was on full display. "Get a good view?" she asked and turned to secure it.

"We're taking off. Now. Get in your seat," he

grumbled.

"What? No 'please'?" She raised her eyebrows as she moved toward her chair and glanced at the seat. "My bag!"

"Unless you want to be plastered to the wall, I'd take a seat and buckle up now, Princess," Walker said while Benjamin closed and locked the door before taking his seat behind his boss.

She flopped into her seat and clicked the seatbelt over her lap. Her fingertips ran over the side of her bag like it was a talisman connecting Stacia to her real life. The one in LA that didn't include brooding thugs and luxury private jets. "How'd you get my bag back?" She shot him a sidelong look as he secured himself into the chair across the cabin. She checked her wallet. The credit cards and even cash were all undisturbed. She rummaged through the rest of her bag. "My phone. Where's my phone?"

"You'll get it back when you're home," he said as his thumb slid over his own phone.

Her shoulders relaxed slightly, and she leaned back in the seat as the jet's motor came to life. *Home.* She'd be going home eventually. Her eyes flew open as a thought popped into her head. "Did you kill him?" she asked, her voice growing louder over the motor.

Walker either didn't hear her or chose not to answer. She was sure it was the latter. Stacia was about to ask again when the jet propelled forward and built up speed so quickly, her body molded to the seat and she couldn't pick her head off the headrest if she tried as she white-knuckled the armrests. A religious person she wasn't, but at that moment she sent a silent prayer to any spirit who cared to listen as the wheels left the ground and they were airborne. She hadn't a clue where they were headed, but somehow, she knew she was in protective, but dangerous, hands.

Chapter Three

Benjamin was the first to rise from his seat after the plane leveled off and the roar of the motor quieted to a gentle purr. "Can I get you something to drink, Stacia?"

"Bottle of water if you have it." Benjamin produced a bottle from the refrigerator at the small bar in front of the cabin. "Thanks." The word came out as a squeak, and she cleared her throat.

Benjamin handed Walker a highball glass of something clear over ice after Walker pulled his massive body from the chair and sauntered across the cabin. Her flesh buzzed when his gaze caressed Stacia as he leaned against the wall directly in front of her chair, appearing even more like a mass of muscle. Her gaze shifted to his hand. "A little early for the hard stuff, isn't it?"

The ice cubes tinkled against the glass as he gave it a swirl. "If club soda serves as hard stuff then no. It's not too early."

She pointed to her bag on the floor near Walker's feet. "How'd you get my bag back?"

"I heard your question the first time."

She leaned forward. "You didn't answer the first time. You also didn't tell me if you killed him?"

"Did I kill whom?" The corner of his mouth hitched up in an almost half smile. That was a first.

He was toying with her, and she didn't like it. "You know damn well who I'm talking about. Jake. Is he dead? Is that how you got my bag back? Everything is still in it, except for my phone, which I assume you have. Even the cash was there."

A low chuckle erupted from his throat. "Jake wasn't interested in pocketing your sixty-seven dollars. He wanted something else from you."

Heat rose in her cheeks as she flipped off her

seatbelt and stood. "I know he didn't take me to Las Vegas to rob me of a few dollars. I'm not stupid." She moved to the bar to look for something, well, stronger. Not because she wanted it but because she needed a reason to detach herself from his gaze.

"You're hardly stupid, Princess."

She opened a cabinet, and a row of wine bottles gleamed back. She examined the labels and chose a Silver Oak Cabernet Sauvignon. "Since you've gone to great lengths to learn so much about me, I'd appreciate it if you'd use my name," she said as she searched for a corkscrew.

"Allow me." Benjamin swept to her side, took the bottle from her hands and produced a corkscrew seemingly out of thin air.

"Thank you." She watched as Benjamin opened the bottle and poured her a glass, not missing the sideways look he tossed Walker's way along with a nod in her direction.

Walker cleared his throat. "Forgive me, Stacia. You wanted to know if I killed Jake. You'll be happy to know he's alive and well."

"I wouldn't say I'm happy about it," she said, accepting the glass from Benjamin.

"You wanted me to kill him?"

She considered his question as she lifted the glass to her nose and inhaled. "No. Maybe rough him up a little." After all, if what Walker said was true. Jake's orders were to kill her, but she certainly didn't want to be the reason someone lost their life. That would've been hell on her conscience.

"That was the plan," he muttered.

She tilted her head. "He got away? Is that why you were stressed out before we took off?"

"You're observant."

"Occupational hazard. I wondered what had you hot and bothered?" Her heart drummed in her chest as his gaze melted slowly over her body.

He took a sip from his glass without breaking his stare. "I was disappointed Jake slipped away before we had the chance to question him. But I'm confident he'll make himself available soon."

"You seem pretty sure of that."

"He screwed up. A couple times. First when you left the suite undetected. Next when I found you before he did. He works for a powerful man who's not pleased with him right now. He's going to need to make it right."

She shook her head. "I don't get it. Who is he?"

"Jake's one of Carlo Cardinelli's newer soldiers."

"Cardinelli? As in the mob family?" The fact Jake was planning to kill her suddenly made sense.

"Who'd you think you were dealing with?"

"Not the mafia," she spat. "Why would I fly to Vegas with a mobster?"

"That question crossed my mind. Tell me what you know about him."

Stacia took a long sip from her glass. *Here we go.* She'd wondered when he'd start the interrogation. "Don't you mean tell you what I know about Platinum?"

His mouth quirked, but he didn't say a word. They stood a few feet from each other in silence. Stacia knew his tactic. Silence was the first lesson of Reporting 101. Most people try to fill moments of awkward silence with words. The first person to speak loses the advantage.

"Platinum," he repeated.

Advantage Stacia. She straightened her back. "I presume that's who you work for. Name's on the plane. Why don't you cut the shit and ask me what you really want to know?"

His eyes locked with hers, but she refused to look away. "Why did you go to Vegas with a man you didn't know?"

"For a story that would've jumpstarted my career."

"What story?"

"The only thing he'd say was it was about Platinum, that he was a disgruntled employee who wanted to get even. He hinted there was something going on in the sudden crop of clubs Platinum opened, like The Silver Club in Vegas. He said if I joined him at the opening of the club I'd get my story."

"The Silver Club isn't Platinum's. It's owned by the Cardinellis."

She shook her head. "I did my research. Platinum bought the property."

"You didn't finish your homework. Platinum bought it but resold it to Carlo Cardinelli."

"It must've been recent because it didn't show up on my search." She tilted her head. "The real question is why would a security and national defense company buy a nightclub and sell it to a known mobster?"

Ice cubes clinked against his glass as he gave it another swirl. "It was necessary. Dealing with Carlo is a calculated game of give and take. We may have given him the club, but today we took you."

"It still doesn't make sense. And if it's a Cardinelli club, why would they risk turning the attention on themselves?"

"Not sure, but Jake's job was to lure you there for some reason."

"Why me? If exposure was what they were after wouldn't they contact a reporter with more clout?" Stacia had no doubt she would be one of those reporters in time, but as a junior reporter she still had to beg for fluff pieces.

"They wanted someone green because they knew you'd keep it quiet. You'd want the story for yourself."

She leaned against the cabin wall and closed her eyes, angry for letting her drive for success overshadow common sense. She'd played right into Jake like an idiot.

"What happened at the hotel before you left?" Walker asked.

Stacia rubbed her forehead as she tried to recall the details of the last moments in the Vegas hotel suite. "We checked into adjoining suites. I didn't want connecting rooms but he insisted and said I could lock my side, so I agreed. I noticed the adjoining door was open when I was getting dressed for dinner. He must've been in my room when I was in the shower. So, I marched over to his side to rip him a new asshole and heard him on the phone in the bedroom. He said he had me and if I gave him trouble he'd take care of it. I realized I was in over my head and no one knew where I was. So I went back to my suite and left." She paused, realizing how she'd let her ambition cloud her common sense. "You must think I'm stupid."

"I didn't say that."

"But you're thinking it."

"You didn't tell anyone where you were going? Your boss? Your father?"

She shook her head. "I knew my boss wouldn't agree on it, so I took a couple days off and went on my own time. I figured if I came back with the story, I'd be a rock star. You know the saying: ask for forgiveness, not permission. Taking chances is part of the business. It was the chance I took."

"What about your father? Why didn't you tell him you were going to Vegas?"

Stacia gazed out the window. "My father believes

in doing things by the book. He wouldn't understand. He's not pleased with my career choice, and he hates Las Vegas, almost as much as he hates LA."

"Your father sounds like a smart man."

Her father was a brilliant man. General Howell reminded her of that fact with every wrong move she made. If he had it his way she would've gone to law school and joined a practice in Cleveland.

Walker drained his glass and placed it on the counter. "Look, I don't know why they lured you to Vegas, but it wasn't to break open some story. There isn't one to report."

"Maybe. But there is one now."

He pinned her with a heavy stare. "There's no story."

She chuckled. "I'm being kidnapped by one of this country's most powerful and mysterious corporations and there's no story? Bull. Shit."

Chapter Four

Walker ran his palm over his jaw. She was unlike any woman he'd known. He was used to two types of women during questioning, the criers, and those who wanted to get him in bed. Stacia wasn't either one, although he wouldn't mind the latter. She was calm and cool, and even though he caught her checking out his own assets, he doubted she would be an easy conquest. He couldn't pry his eyes off her curves, but if another foul word fell from her pretty lips he'd have a hard time resisting the urge to bend her over and spank her round ass. He flexed his fingers and strode to the chair she'd occupied during takeoff. Releasing the lock, he swiveled it to face the one behind it.

"Take a seat," he said, buying a few seconds to collect his thoughts and expel the mental picture of his hand mark on her backside.

Stacia Howell would be more of a challenge than he'd originally thought, but he was certainly up for the task. She sat, crossing one long leg over the other as he settled into the other seat and met her stare. "Okay. We'll do it your way." Which was a lie. Women like Stacia liked to think they had the upper hand. He'd let her think she so, but Walker knew better. "You think you have a story. Tell me what you know about Platinum?"

She took another sip while maintaining eye contact. He knew she was also deciding her course of action. Perhaps deciding what she was ready to say now and what to keep in her back pocket. He knew the game. Shit, he'd invented the game.

She leaned forward, and her eyes danced like they held a secret. "Platinum is a privately held security and defense company holding billion-dollar contracts with the government. But their recent focus is on the hospitality market. They're buying up failing resort properties in the US and Caribbean."

He shrugged. "Nothing newsworthy about that."

"Not on the surface, but the resorts close for extensive remodels and they don't reopen to the public."

"So?"

"They're being used as private clubs. At least that's the official word from the press release," she said with a hint of an eyeroll.

"That's true. Platinum saw a need for niche luxury travel. These properties fill that need." It was the official prepared statement, which he was sure she'd read.

She held her half full glass in her hand and rested her elbows on her knees. Her hair tumbled over her left shoulder. Walker shifted in his seat, unable to pull his gaze from her wine-stained lips. "That's a bunch of bullshit, and you know it," she said.

He rubbed his palms together as an image of his palm on her ass flashed in his head. "Since you think you know more about Platinum than I do, tell me. What do *you* think the clubs are used for?"

"I don't know exactly. It's what I'd hoped to find out in Vegas."

"You don't seem like the type to follow a strange man to Vegas based on an unsubstantiated tip." Stacia Howell wasn't a pushover. That fact was evident in the detailed report Benjamin pulled on her, and it was obvious in the way she'd dealt with her present situation. The woman had balls of steel. Unfortunately, those balls almost rolled right into the wrong hands.

She set her glass on the ledge under the window and bit the nail of her right index finger. He'd seen her do it in the car while her mind was seemingly racing in a million directions. "It would be the story of the year."

"And you wanted it."

"Hell, yes." She leaned forward. "I still do."

"That's quite a tale, but I think you're leaving out the best part."

"What would that be?"

A smile crossed his lips. "You tell me."

He watched her neck work as she swallowed. "Jake mentioned one of the reasons the resorts weren't open to the public was they catered to sexual deviancy."

Now they were getting somewhere. "That interested you?" he asked, enjoying the warm blush spreading from her neck to her cheeks.

"For the story." She shrugged. "Sex sells."

"For the story," he repeated. "Benjamin, would you give me the file on Ms. Howell, please?"

Benjamin placed a leather folder on the table next to Walker. However, he didn't need it. Walker knew exactly what was in the report. He'd read it countless times. Her gaze landed on the folder. "What's that?"

"Research on you." He picked up the leather packet and flipped it open. "You seem to like to do a lot of online investigation."

"It's part of my job." She shifted in her chair.

"You've been interested in bondage lately." He narrowed his eyes. "Is your network planning a special report on kink? Sounds like a great dinner hour spot."

Her eyes zeroed in on his. "How long have you been spying on me?"

He smiled. Stacia Howell landed on Walker's radar a couple weeks ago when the Platinum agent assigned to keep tabs on Jake noted her as a person of interest. Walker was drawn to her as soon as he viewed her handful of on-air network spots. Her smoky eyes held a story, and he wasn't at all surprised when he discovered her interests. "Long enough to know what you're about,

Stacia."

Fire flashed through her gaze, but it was gone as fast as it appeared. She squared her shoulders. "You're reading more into it. That research was strictly for my job. Let's get back to how much of the information Jake gave me is true about Platinum?"

He studied her face. She was like a damn piranha trying to sink her teeth into a story he wasn't about to divulge. "None of it."

"Doubt that. There's always a seed of truth in a field of lies."

"Walker." Benjamin signaled him from his seat on the other side of the cabin.

He stood, strode to Benjamin, and raised his brows.

"There's a storm over Miami. The pilot wants to know if you're okay with diverting to one of the Caribbean properties?"

Walker glanced at Stacia. His plan was to keep her at Platinum's newly opened Miami resort until Jake resurfaced and it was safe to send her home. Suddenly he didn't see the need to get rid of her right away. In fact, he knew exactly where he wanted her. It was a risk, but it was one he was willing to take. "No. I don't think so. Tell him to gain clearance to land in New Orleans."

Benjamin's gaze bounced from Walker to Stacia and back to his employer. "Prytania House isn't finished yet," he said in a hushed voice.

Walker recalled the details of the project manager's last status report. "It's livable for a few days until Jake crawls out of his hole. Have a car waiting for us on the tarmac and provisions brought to the house before we get there. I don't want anyone to see her. We can't risk a leak."

"What about security?" Benjamin asked.

"The exterior is locked tighter than the National Bank."

"It's not the exterior I'm talking about," Benjamin said in a low voice.

Walker's heart drummed in his chest. "Get the paperwork ready and I'll manage Ms. Howell's access within the house." Walker checked his watch and did a quick time calculation. "Get on it. We should have another hour of flight time to New Orleans," he said and turned toward Stacia.

Her eyes were on him as he returned to his seat. "There's been a change in plans."

"Does that mean you're going to tell me where we're going?"

He studied her eyes and caught a flicker of worry. The change from the Miami resort to Prytania House meant he'd have to change his strategy with Stacia as well. He'd have to earn her trust. He nodded. "Yes. We'll land in New Orleans shortly."

"New Orleans? I don't remember reading about a Platinum property in New Orleans."

She'd done her homework on Platinum, but the New Orleans property wasn't an asset of the company. It was privately owned, but he wasn't about to show all his cards yet. "It's a new acquisition. Prytania House is a unique property, but it's top secret so I need your confidentiality. You can't report on the place nor anything you see or experience inside."

"What if I don't agree?"

He shrugged. "You'll have to stay on the plane until I figure out what to do with you." He'd hoped that wouldn't be the case.

Her eyes scanned her surroundings, and he'd bet the price of the jet she was dying to continue the adventure. "Fine. You have my word."

"Unfortunately, that's not good enough." Benjamin appeared at his side with contract and pen in hand. "I'll need you to sign this."

"What is it?"

"An NDA. Non-discl— "

Her eyes flashed again. "A non-disclosure agreement. I know what that is. You don't trust me?"

He considered her question, which he couldn't answer. Not yet. However, he'd know soon. "It's business, and it's non-negotiable. Sign it and join me at Prytania House. Refuse and stay on board. It's that simple. I'll let Benjamin review the details of the contract with you."

He felt her stare on his back as he moved to the other end of the cabin. He leaned his palms on the ledge, his face within a few inches of the window. After a few minutes, a flash of silver drew his attention to the reflection in the glass as she signed the form with Benjamin's pen.

Chapter Five

Walker remained on the other side of the cabin for the rest of the flight, which annoyed her even more. She was still heated after he bullied her into signing the NDA. There was no way she'd stay cooped up on the jet for fuck knows how long. She turned toward the window as the plane began its descent into what looked to be a private airport. She clicked her seatbelt and leaned back in her seat surveying the landscape as the plane touched down.

After they landed, Walker talked quietly on his phone while Benjamin opened the door before gesturing to Stacia. As she walked by, she gave Walker a side eye glare, which he ignored. Stacia followed Benjamin off the jet. She stood on the platform of the stairs as the moist air hit her like a wet towel.

"We have to keep moving." Benjamin grabbed her hand and led her to the waiting car at the bottom of the stairs. It was like a scene straight out of a movie, and it wasn't the first time Stacia wondered if she was in a crazy dream. Benjamin shuttled her into the backseat and closed the door before moving to the other side of the car and taking a seat behind the wheel. Walker slid in and the car jolted forward as he slammed the door.

The scenery raced by in a blur as Benjamin zigzagged through the streets. She gripped the door handle during a sharp turn. "Jeez, it's good thing we haven't eaten. Where'd you learn to drive, Benjamin?" she called over the seat.

"Ever been to New Orleans?" Walker asked.

"I lived here for a while. I've lived everywhere. Army brat." Stacia's thoughts turned to her father. She'd moved countless times throughout her childhood. It had been only the two of them for as long as she could remember. Her mother had died when Stacia was only three.

They came to a stop at a light, and her gaze fell on the gates of a cemetery. Moss-covered cement boxes lined up in rows like they were forgotten vessels from another era. She remembered learning about the tombs of New Orleans and why they're placed above ground because of the low water table. She used to wake up crying from dreams about the dead bodies coming to life. But she received little comfort from her father. Nightmares were a sign of weakness as far as General Howell was concerned. He treated Stacia much like he did his military unit—with cold authority. The car veered to the right, jolting Stacia from the past. Finally, they slowed as she took in dense greenery in front of stately homes. "We're in the Garden District," she remarked.

He nodded. "You do know the area."

"I lived in Baton Rouge as a teenager and I'd sneak into New Orleans every chance I could, which was hardly ever."

The car stopped in front of a gate, and the metal bars parted before they entered a lush courtyard with flowering trees and bushes. They pulled alongside the house, and Stacia stepped out of the car. Scanning the shaded courtyard, she inhaled the aroma of honeysuckle as birds chirped in the distance. She took another breath and let it out slowly as a calm settled over her body. Her gaze moved to the gingerbread style Victorian mansion. The black shutters and white trim were perfect accessories for the deep red tone of the house's siding. A wrought-iron wraparound railing showcased a stately front porch.

"It's beautiful," she muttered. It was different from the small utilitarian type houses she had lived in most of her life.

Walker moved to her side. "The interior's still rough. The house is under renovation so it's not fully functional. There are certain rooms that are off limits." He turned toward the car as Benjamin closed the driver's side door. "All clear?" Walker asked.

"Clear," Benjamin responded.

"What does that mean?" Stacia asked.

"The house has a multi-layered security system. Benjamin digitally disarmed the system so we can enter." He waved his hand toward the door.

"Ever hear of a key?" Stacia asked as the door opened and she peered inside. Based on Walker's description of the high-tech security system, she'd expected a modern decor. Instead, it was as if she were entering a well-appointed late eighteen-hundreds Victorian mansion. She took a step inside onto a gleaming dark wood floor. The room could've come straight out of a movie. A polished wood and upholstered settee, with matching high-back chairs, faced the enormous, intricately carved wood fireplace. She caught her reflection in the mirror above the mantel, and her gaze shifted over her shoulder to Walker. "This is rough?"

The corners of his eyes crinkled as he grinned. It was the first genuine smile she'd seen on him. He strode to the middle of the creamy area rug covering much of the floor. "Looks better than the last time I was here. Upstairs isn't finished yet. I'll take you on a tour."

They moved from room to room on the main floor beginning in the dining room, then shifting to the library, and the staff sleeping quarters, which were larger than her whole apartment. "And the kitchen," he said surveying the contents of the refrigerator. "Something to drink?"

Stacia shook her head, picked up an apple from

the bowl of fruit on the granite countertop, and brought it to her nose. She placed it back and narrowed her eyes. "No one lives here?"

"It's vacant at the moment."

"There are a lifetime of books in the library, enough food for a party in here, and the rest looks like the setting for Scarlett O'Hara's tea party. This isn't what a vacant house looks like."

"Platinum runs an efficient staff. I requested the house be prepared for visitors and provisions were brought in," he said, dismissing her comment.

Benjamin strode into the kitchen. "The rest of the items you requested arrived for Ms. Howell. Should I put them in the spare staff bedroom?"

"No. I'd like her things moved upstairs. I believe one of the guest bedrooms is almost finished."

Stacia's gaze bounced from Benjamin to Walker as the men stared at each other. "Very well," Benjamin said with a slight nod and left.

Walker jerked his head toward the door. "I'll show you the rest."

She shrugged and plucked the apple from the bowl and took a bite. The sweet and tangy juice ran over her tongue. It was probably the best apple she'd ever tasted. She imagined what steps his staff had taken procuring the best of the best in the short time period they were given. She shook her head. For the moment, she'd go with it. She was safe and from the looks of their provisions, would be well fed. She swallowed and waved her palm. "Lead the way."

Chapter Six

Walker had considered taking Benjamin's advice and restricting Stacia's access to the first floor by having her stay in the empty staff quarters. It was the plan, and Walker never deviated from a plan. This was a rare exception. There was something about her that made him want to toss his rigid procedures into the wind and board the wild ride of Stacia Howell. He stepped aside at the bottom of the curved staircase. "Ladies first."

"Why? You want to check out my ass?" she huffed and bumped her hip into his thigh as she moved forward.

"Actually, I'd like to see your reaction as you go upstairs." His view was a bonus.

He watched her fingertips brush the top of the banister as she ascended the staircase. Even her most innocent actions overloaded him with images that had no business inside his head. She gasped when she reached the top step, eliciting yet another X-rated idea of how he could coax more sounds from her lips. He cleared his throat, regaining his composure as he moved to her side.

"I'd hoped for that response." He followed her gaze to the long row of stained glass windows along the wall. The late afternoon sun shone through the glass, casting vivid hues on the landing.

She carefully approached and touched an index finger to one of the panes. "Amazing. Are they original?"

He crossed his arms and watched her examine the scenes. "Some of them are. Most were damaged beyond salvage over the years so they were reproduced," he explained.

Her gaze flicked to each. "They're abstracts of women's bodies in various acts of sex, correct?"

"You have a good eye. Most people don't see it at

first. They notice only shapes and colors."

Her gaze held on one window, his favorite. "I definitely see it. These are scenes of bondage," she said, unabashed.

"Correct again."

"They're incredible." They stood in silence for a few moments as she studied the two-story wall showcasing the colorful glass artwork. "Together the scenes seem to tell a story as they continue up the wall." He followed her gaze up the narrow circular staircase leading to the tower. "It's a woman's journey through the experience." Her gaze flicked to Walker before moving back to the first pane. "Here, she's detached. She's on one side of the scene. On the outside looking in." Her pointed index finger moved from window to window as she followed the story. "As the woman progresses deeper into the world the colors start to blend and become richer. The experience sets her free of the boundaries holding her back." Her voice softened. "It helps her soar."

He'd never known someone who understood the meaning of the window scenes like she did. He wondered if they touched her even more than they did to himself. He moved closer. So close the heat of her arm ghosted over his own. "Tell me how that could happen if she is bound the way she is there." He pointed to one of the last scenes at the top.

Her gaze caught the pane he identified. "Physical bonds aren't meant to be confining. They're a symbol of trust and a tool to help the person focus on what they're feeling, not on their actions. By freeing the person of the act of decision making, you're allowing them to place their pleasure into trusted hands. Is there anything more empowering than that?"

Walker hadn't realized he held his breath as she

described what had been ingrained in him for most of his life. "Not many people surprise me, but you just did."

They stood in silence for a long moment, both lost in their own thoughts.

She shook her head slightly and turned to Walker. "What's on the third floor?"

He resisted the urge to allow her into his world, but it was too soon. He didn't want to frighten her. However, he was almost certain she wouldn't be afraid. Still, she wasn't ready. "The Tower Room."

"May I see it?"

He shook his head. "Off limits. It's still under construction."

She turned to him and opened her mouth to speak but closed it again and turned back toward the wall. "So these are originals and copies of originals. They must be over a hundred years old."

"This house was built in the eighteen-sixties. I have pictures of the windows dating back to nineteen-twenty."

Her eyes sparkled. "Man, if this house could only talk. What do you know about the previous owners?"

"I have some information you'll find interesting I'll share with you at dinner. Want to see your room?"

Stacia's eyes flicked back to the staircase before landing on him again. "My room? Sounds like this is for more than a couple days. How long do you plan to keep me here?"

For as long as it takes. "Until we locate Jake and get more information."

She put her hand on her hip, and Walker's gaze rested on the curve of her waist. "How long's this going to take? I need to get back to work. I have deadlines."

He raised his hand. "Don't worry about work. They know you'll be out for a few days."

"You called my office?"

"Benjamin did. It's taken care of."

"You had no right to do that. You're taking over my life, and there's not a damn thing I can do about it," she huffed. "And since you have all the answers, then answer me this… What's going to happen when I return with a story I can't even report thanks to the NDA you bullied me into signing?" Stacia threw her hands up.

He enjoyed watching her frustration and decided to add fuel to the fire. "I didn't bully you into anything. You didn't have to sign it."

"I wasn't about to sit in that tin can for days on end." Her manicured finger poked his chest. "You gave me no choice."

He grabbed her index finger and held it tight in his fist. "You had a choice, and so did I. I chose to bring you here, and you chose to come. Every choice we make comes with risks and benefits. Remember that. As far as the story, you'll have one. Just not the one you thought you'd have."

She pulled her hand away and folded her arms. "You think you're going to feed me a story for Platinum's benefit? Think again. I don't work that way."

He stepped back and mimicked her stance. "I don't either. I promise you'll have a legitimate story to report."

"Why should I believe you?" She raised her brows in challenge.

Walker pushed from the railing he leaned against and took a couple paces until he was directly in front of her. She squared her shoulders. Her chin rose as she maintained eye contact. She was tougher than most of the Platinum agents he worked with. She'd be hard to break, but he had never backed down from a challenge. "You'll have to trust me."

"Why should I?"

He lowered his face to hers and closed the space between, coming within an inch of her skin. His gaze lingered on her lips before he tilted his face so his mouth was over her ear. "Because I can help you soar," he said in a low voice deliberately using her own words. He pulled away, and her eyes told him everything he needed to know about Stacia. She was so much like him, but he'd known that already. He knew that the moment he pulled the recordings and saw the fire in her eyes. But it was a bold move on his part and a stupid one. He should stay away from her at least until he knew how she was involved with the Cardinellis and what they wanted from Stacia.

He tore his gaze from her and placed his hand at the small of her back, guiding her down the hall to her room. A pang of disappointment ran through his head when he pushed it open and assessed the room. The small guest bedroom was lacking the luxury of most of the rooms in the house since he hadn't expected visitors. A bed with a simple upholstered headboard, nightstand, chest of drawers, and a freestanding full-length mirror completed the room. Maybe he should've put her in the staff quarters after all. "I didn't realize how unfinished the second floor is. We can move you downstairs."

She waved off his offer. "It's fine. Really," she said. "You should see my apartment. It's about the same size."

"Take a look at the clothes Benjamin ordered for you and let him know if you need anything else. There should be toiletry items in the bathroom, too. He'll get you anything else you need."

Their gazes met, and he knew their minds weren't on the size of the bedroom or what was in the closet. Her thoughts were still on the stained-glass scenes. He could almost see her body reacting to it, which sent an electric current racing through his body straight to his cock. He never should've brought her to the second floor. He should've listened to Benjamin and kept her contained downstairs. In fact, he should've left her on the plane. He swallowed hard. "Dinner's at seven," he muttered on his way out the door.

Chapter Seven

Stacia scanned the bedroom, which suddenly seemed bigger without Walker's hulking presence. The man sucked up time and space. It was as though she ditched reality in Las Vegas and was transported into the world of Walker. She opened the closet and a soft light illuminated a row of clothing and shoes. She pulled a few hangers from the rod and examined the garments. If a stylist had picked out her dream wardrobe with a sky's the limit budget, it would look very much like the closet's contents. At least she'd be well-dressed while living in Walker's world. Stacia stepped to the bathroom, also stocked with all her favorite products. She turned the knob of the soaking tub and added a few drops of scented bath oil before striping off her clothes and sinking into the warm water.

She didn't remember the last time she'd taken a bath. Life had taken over, and her days were filled with deadlines and climbing the proverbial career ladder. She smiled. It took getting kidnapped by a sexy stranger and held captive in a nineteenth century mansion for her to have a moment to relax. Stacia laid her head against a towel and sank her shoulders into the lavender-scented water as her mind floated back to the scenes so brazenly displayed in this house that belonged in some erotic fairy tale. Thanks to his stalking resources, Walker knew her curiosity for … what? Kink? It felt like more than that. Most of her online exploration was in search of a label for what she craved. What she needed. However, she learned it wasn't as simple as reading a description and attaching a name. The only way to truly understand it was to experience it with someone who could guide her through the journey. She closed her eyes and let the hot water envelop her body.

****

The bath and a short nap energized Stacia, and she was ready for answers. Dressed casually in a pair of jeans and a silk cami, which, just like the clothes presented to her on the jet, were magically her style and size, she headed downstairs for dinner with a list of questions. As soon as she stepped into the dining room an acrid odor attacked her nostrils.

"I told you it was in too long." Walker's voice carried from the kitchen.

Stacia stood in the doorway as a heavy veil of smoke swirled above her head. Benjamin, donning two oven mitts, grabbed either side of a roasting pan and removed a charred hunk of something indistinguishable from the oven. "Smells delicious," she said.

Both men turned to her. "Neither one of us are chefs," Walker said with a sneer in Benjamin's direction.

"I can see that." She pointed to the pan. "Mind if I take a peek?"

Benjamin placed the pan on the stove, and the three of them stared at the black crusted brick. She picked up a fork from the counter and poked the charred block of what was probably a great cut of meat. "There's no saving it," she said, glancing in the pantry. She spotted a box of pasta and a jar of sauce. "Got any chopped beef?"

"I think there's a package in the fridge," Benjamin said.

"Perfect." She grabbed the items and shooed Walker and Benjamin from the kitchen. She was far from a great chef, but she could manage spaghetti and meatballs.

She set a couple of pots on the stove, filling one with water for the pasta. A calmness settled over her body, and she found herself relishing the mundane task of preparing dinner. At least it kept her from focusing on her present situation.

Stacia pulled open the drawers under the counter two at a time in search of a large spoon. "Where do you keep—" she called out but stopped mid-sentence as her eyes landed on the black remote control. She hadn't noticed a television screen in the house, which made her extra curious about the remote. She picked it up and brushed her thumb over the buttons until it rested on a red circle. A moment after she tapped it, a motor sounded from above her head. Her gaze moved to the ceiling where a screen slowly emerged and illuminated the same time Walker and Benjamin rushed into the kitchen. Her gaze moved from the screen to the men.

"That's pretty cool. Is it hooked up to cable?" Her eyes darted back to the monitor where two icons appeared labeled "surveillance" and "entertainment". She randomly poked a couple more buttons, and a series of pictures popped up. Most of them were of the exterior but a few depicted shots from inside the house including the kitchen where she spotted the three of them in one of the squares. However, her attention landed on another interior shot. The room was devoid of furniture except for a massive four-poster bed and a wood cabinet. She hadn't recalled seeing the room on the tour Walker had given her earlier, which meant it must be a shot of the Tower Room, the off limits third floor level. She stepped forward to get a better look, and the remote was ripped from her hand. She turned as Walker hit one of the buttons and a news program flashed on the screen.

"Are you interested in watching something in particular?" he asked.

"Um. I…" The vision of the bed clouded her head. "What was that?"

"The house is wired for security cameras."

"So I saw. I understand the outside cameras, but you have them inside, too? Is there a camera in my bedroom?"

His ocean blue eyes were like lasers capturing her gaze. "There aren't cameras in any of the bedrooms."

She pointed at the screen. "But, I saw—"

"Did you want to watch something, Stacia?" Benjamin's voice boomed from across the room.

She tipped her glance in Benjamin's direction. A flicker of warning flashed in his eyes. She opened her mouth to argue but decided against it. She'd play by Walker's rules, for now. "KCLA's afternoon news is on. Want to flip it on while I finish dinner?" she asked, forcing a smile.

"I'm sure we get it. We have all the major news markets. Let's see…" Benjamin busied himself with the remote flipping through channels while Stacia found a ladle in another drawer. Her gaze landed on Walker watching her intently. She ignored him as she surveyed the assorted bottles of spices, but the image of the massive bed burned hot in her mind. "Here it is."

Benjamin's words moved her focus back to the screen where the newscast's anchors reported on LA politics. She kept her eye on the monitor as she moved around the kitchen. Stacia assumed Walker and Benjamin remained in the room to ensure she didn't nosily flip the remote to surveillance mode. They took a seat at the counter, and she put them to work on slicing vegetables for the salad. From the outside, the scene had appeared as normal meal preparation, but she knew their minds were on anything but the ordinary. She was about to mention the big, fat elephant in the room when her own version of the elephant appeared on the screen in the form of a platinum blonde bombshell.

"I had the opportunity to attend the star-studded

premiere of…"

A lump formed in Stacia's throat. She raised her hand to the screen. "Turn it off."

Benjamin poked the remote that sat on the counter between Walker and himself as though they were guarding the crown jewels of the Queen of England. Both men seemed relieved when the screen retracted into the ceiling.

Walker raised an eyebrow. "Something wrong?"

She slammed the spoon on the counter and sauce spattered over the marble surface. "Oh nothing. Just that while I'm here playing Mama Leone, Tiffany Connor took my assignment."

"So?" Walker shrugged.

"It took me five years before I got screen time while little miss big tits moved from fetching coffee to interviewing stars in five seconds flat. She was hired as an intern a few months ago. I worked hard for the little bit of air time I get and Tiffany bats her fake eyelashes at some producer's pants, and there she is." Stacia waved her hand in the direction of where the screen disappeared. "I wonder who she's fucking?"

"Is that how you got your break?" Walker asked in his even tone, but she couldn't help noticing his jaw clench.

She narrowed her eyes. "Did you hear what I said? I worked for my break. Not sucked cock for it."

She watched him set his hands on the counter and his fingers turned white as they pressed into the marble. He pushed the chair back with force as he stood, sending it crashing to the floor before he sauntered out.

"What's wrong with him?" Stacia jerked her chin toward the door.

Benjamin chuckled as he bent to pick up the chair. He righted the chair and pushed it into place at the counter. "Walker is not a fan of beautiful women using vulgar language."

Stacia blinked. "You're kidding. He's pissed because I have a potty mouth?" She wasn't sure if she should be concerned or laugh. Then it occurred to her he'd called her beautiful. That label wasn't thrown her way much in her line of work. Sure, she was passable in an ordinary way. No one had ever mistaken her dark hair, which she usually wore in a messy bun, and athletic build for a beauty queen by any stretch of the imagination.

"Something like that. Dinner almost ready? Walker may've lost his appetite, but I'm starving," Benjamin said.

She was relieved Benjamin made light of the situation. One brooding man was enough to deal with. Stacia handed him a bottle she pulled from the stocked wine fridge. "Open this and I'll plate the pasta."

She placed a heaping bowl of spaghetti and meatballs in front of Benjamin before filling her own. Benjamin's eyes grew big. "I can't believe you whipped this up."

She tilted her head. "You mean to tell me the fact that I can make a great Italian dinner wasn't noted in that folder of yours? I'm curious. If you can't cook, why didn't you order out?"

"Too risky. We need to limit exposure," he said, uncorking the bottle of Cabernet Sauvignon.

"No news on Jake?" she asked.

"We're getting close. Shouldn't be long."

She hoped he was right and she'd be able to return to her life soon. For now, she'd make the most of the adventure. "Walker mentioned he had information about the previous owners of this house. He was going to tell me at dinner, but I guess he won't be doing that now. Do you know anything about its history?"

He took a sip of wine and nodded. "The house has a sordid past. It'd been a private club for elite New Orleans residents during Prohibition. It was also a brothel. The last owner was a wealthy recluse who enjoyed the company of beautiful women. He did much of the restoration before he died."

"Interesting. That explains the windows upstairs." She twirled her pasta with her fork, debating whether to broach the next subject with Benjamin. She figured she'd get backlash from Walker, but she was due to get that anyway. Truth be told, she was looking forward to it. "Tell me about the current owner, Benjamin."

He shrugged. "It's owned by Platinum."

"Is this going to be Mark Platinum's personal retreat?" she asked, her eyes trained on Benjamin's reaction. She detected a slight flinch of his eyebrows before he took another bite and chewed it slowly, seemingly deciding how to answer her question.

"You'll have to direct that line of inquiry to Walker," he said.

"What do you know about Mark Platinum? Have you ever met him?"

"You'll have to direct that line of inquiry to Walker," he repeated.

"It's a simple question," she countered before a muffled chime sounded from Benjamin's direction.

He pulled a phone from the inside pocket of his jacket, poked the screen, and placed it to his ear without saying a word. He nodded once before returning the phone to his pocket. "Walker would like to see you in the garden in fifteen minutes."

She lifted her wineglass and scanned the kitchen, wondering where the camera was hidden. She was tempted to give it the one finger salute but reconsidered after recalling his reaction to her rant. Not because she was frightened of him. Not exactly. However, she figured she'd already pressed her luck for the evening. She pushed her plate away as her stomach clenched in anticipation. Steeling herself with a sip of wine, she would remain cool and collected, even if her insides were a tangled web of knots.

"How long have you worked for him?" Stacia asked, trying to pull as much information as she could out of Walker's right-hand man.

Benjamin stood and collected the plates. "About ten years."

"Ten years, huh? You must have great stories to tell," she said, collecting the glasses.

He stopped and met her gaze. "I'll take care of the dishes. And with all due respect, I have no stories to tell, Stacia."

Stacia shrugged. It was worth a shot. "I guess I'll grab a sweater and meet His Highness in the garden."

On her way to her room, Stacia hesitated at the bottom of the circular staircase leading to the third floor. Her gaze trailed up the intricately carved wood railings. She craned her head to catch a glance of the Tower Room, but all she saw was darkness. She crossed her arms and studied the collection of stained glass windows. The scenes guided the eye toward the ceiling where the staircase ended. She was sure the room was connected to the theme of the sensual and mysterious window scenes and the fleeting look at the monitor in the kitchen confirmed it. After a quick glance toward the main staircase, she grabbed the railing and placed the ball of her foot on the first step and winced when the step creaked under her weight.

Footsteps sounded on the floor below her. "Stacia, Walker's waiting for you," Benjamin called.

"Tell him to keep his shirt on. I'm coming," she

said lowering her foot from the step and heading toward her room. "Control freak," she muttered. An image of a shirtless Walker doing things she only dared to dream about flashed in her mind as she pulled a sweater from a hanger in the closet.

Chapter Eight

Stacia slipped her arms into the sleeves of the sweater and stepped out of the backdoor onto a brick patio surrounded by a greenery covered fence that reached the mansion's second floor windows. A soft glow illuminated the perimeter of the floor. Stacia's eyes adjusted to the dimness, and she spotted Walker seated on a rattan sofa with his elbow resting on the arm and his phone to his ear. Her body warmed as his gaze trickled over her like a fountain. He poked the screen, dropped his phone on the table next to two glasses filled a quarter way with dark ruby liquid, and waved his hand over the cushion beside him on the sofa. A light breeze fluttered the silk camisole over her stomach, and she wrapped the sweater around her body with her arms as she sat. Walker handed her a glass. "Are you cold?" he asked.

"I'm fine. You seem … calmer." She doubted Walker was ever calm, even when asleep, but she couldn't help noticing how his bare ankle peeked from the hem of his pants as he casually crossed it over the knee of his other leg. It was an improvement from knocking over furniture. However, his relaxed posture was in stark contrast to the clipped tone of his voice. She scanned the surroundings. Flowering vines crawled up the posts to the top of the archway over the sitting area. A flame flickered inside the glass hurricane candle holder casting shadows over the patio. "It's beautiful out here. Hard to believe we're in the middle of a neighborhood. It feels like we're the only people for miles."

He held his glass to hers, and she met it with a soft clink. "It was a challenge to secure the garden as tight as the house, but we managed to do it." He took a sip and stared at her intently. "I'm going to ask you a few questions, and I'd like you to answer them honestly."

"I'll answer yours, but I have a few questions of my own."

He tipped his head. "Fair enough but I'll go first. Why didn't you tell me you knew the name of Platinum's owner on the plane when I asked you if you had any other information?"

"Because I didn't have any information, other than a name," she explained.

"You continue to impress me with your research. Few people know the identity of Platinum's owner."

"I didn't uncover it in my research. Jake told me his name. It was what got me on the plane to Vegas. He said I'd get an exclusive story about Platinum's elusive owner and his shady business dealings."

Stacia didn't miss the slight flex of his cheek. "What else did he tell you?"

"That Mark was in Vegas and the resorts he was acquiring were used to hide underage girls he was bringing to the US from Mexico so he can force them into prostitution and pushing drugs on wealthy assholes. It's all he told me, except that Mark protects his privacy to an extreme. There are no pictures found of him anywhere. No public events. He's private. No one knows anything about him." She didn't have time for a full investigation, but a quick scan of her resources turned up nothing about Mark Platinum. It was as though he didn't exist. She searched his eyes. "He's another one of Platinum's secrets. Have you ever seen your boss?"

"Platinum is privately-held. He's not required to disclose anything to the public."

Stacia chuckled. "If you ever decide to get out of the business of kidnapping reporters you'd have a great career in politics the way you evade questions. You know what I think?"

"Please. Enlighten me."

"Judging by this house I bet he's some old coot way past his prime who gets off on kink."

A grin played at his lips. "You certainly have an interesting perspective."

"I'm more curious about your perspective."

"I operate under the same agreement as the NDA you signed. Benjamin does, too, so you can stop grilling him. I will say his privacy isn't only important to him, it's important to his clients. Any breach in security could jeopardize classified military projects."

"What about the underage girls, drugs, and prostitution?"

"I'm sorry to disappoint you, but those claims are unfounded and false."

She ran her finger over the lip of the glass. "You sure about that?"

"Absolutely."

"If that's the case, you should provide me a statement and I'll report your side before false accusations are leaked to the media."

"Spoken like a true reporter. Have you ever heard the saying 'Don't roll in the mud with pigs'?"

"Of course. You're worried Platinum will come out looking dirtier than the enemy?"

He shook his head. "I'm not worried about anything. Given your line of work, I'm sure you don't subscribe to the same belief, but sometimes the best response is no response."

She laughed. "Yeah. I've noticed that about you. Which reminds me, I never got an answer. Is this Mark's place?" she asked, knowing she wouldn't get an answer.

He took a slow sip, and his gaze moved to the brick faced back of the mansion. "My task is to get it finished. Who will occupy it when it's done is yet to be seen. What do you think about the house?"

"What I think is that you're a master spinner. You avoid answering a question by asking another one." She took a sip of port, which slid smoothly down her throat and settled warm in her belly. Her shoulders relaxed as she rolled her head, stretching the kinks from her neck. "Do you succeed in everything you set out to achieve?" she asked.

He uncrossed his legs and rested both elbows on his knees as he cradled the glass in one hand. He rotated the glass in circles and watched the liquid coat the sides and roll back to the bottom. "Most of the time. Do you?"

She shrugged. "I try but not always." She thought of the job she'd wanted in New York. She was fresh out of college with a shiny new Communications degree from a great school and naively assumed the world was at her feet. It was the first of many rejections she'd received until she finally landed a job reporting traffic at a local network in Cleveland. It took a few years before she made it to LA. And she still struggled to get more than fluffy museum openings assignments.

"Why do you think that is?" he asked, his voice husky and warm.

She narrowed her eyes. "That I don't always succeed? I don't know. Lack of experience? Or maybe it's because pretty blondes with big tits get my stories."

He placed his glass on the table and turned to face her. "I've watched you on television and have seen your skills in researching a story. What you think you lack in experience, you make up in knowledge. You're cleverer than reporters with twenty years on the job and tougher than most of the agents I work with."

She was surprised he'd seen her on television. Other than the local traffic gig, she hadn't had many on-camera opportunities with KCLA.

"As far as other reporters getting your stories, it has nothing to do with hair color or body type. There's only one reason you won't achieve everything you put your mind to and that's your lack of confidence. And that stops now. I won't tolerate you putting yourself down."

She glared. "You won't tolerate it? As much as you think you can bully people into doing what you want, you can't force someone to be confident. It comes with age and experience."

His gaze was hot as it washed over her. "Confidence comes with trust and discipline, but you already know that. You've studied it."

"I don't understand." She took another sip, hoping it would slow her heart, which was beating out of control. A warm haze floated over her body, but the liquid encouragement keyed her up even more.

"Your research of bondage and discipline and the Dom/sub lifestyle. You've spent a lot of time learning about it. It draws you."

She swallowed hard, and the fire burning low in her core traveled up to her cheeks. "It was research," she said in almost a whisper.

"There's nothing to be ashamed of, Princess," he said as he stood. Towering over her, he placed his index finger under her chin, tipping her face upward to meet his gaze. "And if I hear you put yourself down again or one more crass word falls from your lips, I'll be forced to give you a taste of what you crave." His thumb traced her bottom lip, and she resisted the desire to open her mouth.

His fiery eyes bored through her for what seemed like an eternity before he dropped his hand to his side. "Good night, Stacia."

He strode to the house leaving Stacia alone on the patio. A gust of wind whipped the ends of her hair around her face as heat raced through her veins and her entire body buzzed with desire.

Chapter Nine

The next morning Walker woke to news Jake had been found. He showered and met Benjamin in the kitchen for a complete report. Benjamin slid a plate piled high with scrambled eggs and bacon in front of Walker and took a seat next to him at the kitchen island.

"At least you didn't burn this," Walker said and nudged his arm with an elbow.

Benjamin nodded toward the sink. "I burned the toast."

Walker spotted the plate of charred toast on the counter. "We got too used to eating out. This is good for us."

Benjamin huffed. "Speak for yourself. You want the briefing?"

"Shoot," Walker said before shoveling a forkful of egg into his mouth.

"They picked Jake up last night. Guess he figured we gave up and he came out of hiding."

"Where'd they grab him?" Walker hoped his men didn't make a scene. Platinum didn't need that type of publicity.

"At the airport. He got out of his cab, and they escorted him into our car. It was quick and easy. No scene," Benjamin said, seemingly anticipating Walker's concern.

"What the hell did he want with Stacia?"

"He said Carlo sent him to use her as a carrot to get to you."

Walker narrowed his eyes. Most mysteries are solved by discovering links. In this case, Stacia wasn't even remotely connected to his world. "Why her?"

Benjamin shook his head. "He claims he doesn't know. He was taking orders from Carlo. He said he figured she was easy prey as a hungry reporter who got suckered in by his charm."

"Bullshit. That doesn't make sense. There's got to be something else." His mind raced as he wrapped his fingers into a fist. He'd been playing a deadly game of chess with Carlo Cardinelli, the head of the largest and deadliest Mafia family, for years. As part of a plan, he'd conceded to Carlo by allowing him to acquire The Silver Club in Vegas, but Carlo seemed to have a plan of his own.

"There's more," Benjamin continued. "Jake said Carlo agreed to leave her alone, but in return he wants—"

"He wants me to leave him alone along with the whole fucking Cardinelli operation."

"Exactly."

"And if I don't?"

"He claims to have evidence that will tie Platinum to their world. The underage prostitution, drug dealing, and trafficking, the whole thing. He'll turn it over to the press."

"And by the time we prove our innocence it'll be too late. The damage will be done."

"Correct," Benjamin confirmed.

"Son of a bitch thinks he has me by the balls." Walker knew Carlo's evidence was weak at best, but any negative news coverage would cause his security and defense clients to pull their contracts. Their clients relied on Platinum's impeccable discretion and confidentiality. Their reputation was at risk for their largest client, the United States Department of Defense. The DoD covertly contracted Platinum to do the dirty work that bordered on legality. It was a risky partnership for Platinum, but a profitable one. However, Walker didn't enter into the contract strictly for the money. Taking Carlo down had become a personal quest.

Benjamin turned to face Walker. "Doesn't he?"

"Not by a long shot." Walker finished his last piece of bacon when a low beep filled his ears.

"She's near the third-floor stairs again. Want me to call her down?" Benjamin asked as he rose from his seat.

Walker waved him off. "Turn on the monitors."

Benjamin reached for the remote on the counter and punched a button, lowering the screen from the ceiling. A dozen boxes popped up, each one showing a different view of the mansion's interior and exterior. Benjamin pushed another button and the frame depicting Stacia enlarged to full screen. Walker watched the monitor as she crept up the stairs while looking over her shoulder every few steps. Walker pointed to the remote. "Switch to the Tower Room cameras."

Benjamin pushed a couple of buttons, and the screen split into two camera views. "Are you sure you want her in there alone?"

"For a few minutes," Walker said quietly as he watched Stacia step inside. She scanned the small room. Her eyes lingered on the leather sectional as she moved to the windows. She pulled the draperies aside and stared at the view for a few moments. She continued around the sofa to the closet on the opposite side of the room. Walker leaned forward as she opened the door and examined the contents and pulled out a bright red corset with black leather lacing. "Where did that come from?"

"I took the liberty of ordering a few Tower Room ensembles for Ms. Howell in case the opportunity arose. I hope it wasn't too forward of me," Benjamin said.

Walker steadied his breath as a fire ignited deep in his stomach. "It was extremely forward of you, Benjamin." He watched as she ran her fingertips down the leather crisscross lacing. "And I owe you for it."

She returned the corset to the closet, closed the door, and moved to the next door, which opened into the room he'd known she'd seen in the monitor the night before. He studied her expression as she moved inside. The interior room was a complete contrast from the first. The soaring ceiling ended with a glass dome showcasing the sky. Sun streamed into the room, casting a warm glow on the otherwise imposing furniture and equipment. She suddenly stopped short like her feet stuck to the ground. He figured she had realized the purpose of the Tower Room. He'd known she'd seen pictures of dungeons during her research, but he'd doubted she'd ever actually visited one. Her chest rose and fell with a deep breath before she walked to the massive four-poster bed. She stood at the foot of the bed and trailed her fingertips up and down the carved pattern on one of the posts, making his body hum with the thought of her touch on his flesh. Her gaze moved to the iron rods that connected each post at the top. She dropped her hand and moved to the front of the bed where she sat on the edge and traced the iron bars that were inset into the polished wood headboard. He was unable to see her face from the camera's angle. The only gauge of her reaction was the steady and slow rise and fall of her back as she breathed.

She stood and used both hands to open the doors of the cabinet next to the bed. A discernible gasp filled his ears as she laid her gaze fixed on the assortment of accessories inside.

"Turn it off," he grumbled at Benjamin. The legs of his chair dragged along the wood floor as he rose. The motor of the screen retracted into the kitchen ceiling as he headed to the second floor. Taking the steps two at a time, he paused when he reached the top, anticipating Stacia's flight from the Tower Room. However, there was no sign of her. He quietly ascended the circular staircase and stepped into the front room. From his vantage, he peered into the other room to see her still standing in front of the open cabinet raking her fingers through the suede blades of one of his favorite floggers.

"I know you're there," she said without turning around. "You were probably watching me the whole time."

Walker cleared his throat. "What makes you think that?" he asked and entered the room.

"Because it took you too long to find me here and I know there are cameras all over this place. Even here." She turned to face him. "Especially here."

He raised his eyebrows in question.

"Isn't that part of this whole thing? The thrill of being watched?" she asked.

He shrugged. "Not necessarily. At least not for me. I prefer a one-on-one connection. It's the reason I don't go to clubs anymore." He leaned against one of the bedposts. "What else do you want to know?"

She pointed the flogger toward the cabinet. "Not gonna lie. Some of this stuff scares the crap out of me. Doesn't it hurt?"

He chuckled softly. "Some of it does, but only when the receiver wants it to hurt."

She paused. "Don't they always?"

"It may seem that way but no."

She narrowed her eyes.

"Let's use this flogger as an example." He held out his hand. She hesitated for a moment before passing it to him.

Gripping the leather handle, he waited for it to become warm and pliable in his hands. He flexed his grip a few times, and the material creaked and popped under his pressure, sending electricity racing through his body.

"Want a demonstration?"

Her glance bounced from him to the flogger in his hand. "Okay," she said after a moment.

Walker pulled open a small drawer in the cabinet and removed a fur-lined blindfold. "I'll explain everything before I do it so there are no surprises. I want you to close your eyes, and I'm going to slide a blindfold over your eyes."

She nodded before closing her eyelids. He scanned her face, assessing her comfort level. The telltale signs of stress were a clenched jaw and rapid breath. Stacia's face was relaxed and her breath even. He lowered the blindfold over her forehead, slowly allowing the fur-lined material to caress her face. "How does that feel?"

"Nice." A small grin passed over her lips.

"I'm going to guide your hand to the bedpost. I want you to hold it lightly for balance." He encircled her left wrist with his left hand and helped her find the post. He dropped the flogger on the bed and placed his right hand on her hip guiding her step so her arm was perpendicular to her body. "Keep your arm straight but don't lock your elbow."

"You're precise."

"Have to be. This isn't something to take lightly. There's a certain respect that must be upheld to ensure there are no accidents."

She nodded once and gripped the post tight.

"Loosen your grip and relax. I'm picking up the flogger now, but I'm not going to touch you with it yet." He rotated the handle in a circle and the blades whooshed in a hushed rhythm. "Do you know why I was watching you in the monitor?"

"No," she said in a breathy tone.

"I wanted to give you the opportunity to explore

on your own. If you didn't like what you saw you could've left and I wouldn't have mentioned it. When your curiosity was obvious, I wanted to see what you'd turn to first. Some people love paddles, some crops, but you were drawn to the flogger, which is one of my favorites."

His body warmed when her grin widened. She was happy it pleased him.

"The flogger can be deceiving. The suede blades can be soft on the skin like a light rain." He swept the ends over her bare forearm, and she shivered. "But each end comes to a point and when used with any degree of force can leave a sting." He flexed his arm and gripped the handle as the ends of the flogger slashed over the edge of the bed. The action startled her, but she kept her stance.

"The dominant partner is always in control of the scene. It's their responsibility to make sure nothing goes wrong, but I'll let you in on a secret. It's the submissive partner that truly holds the power."

"I don't understand."

"You set the limits and decide how far you'll go. Your dominant partner can only push you as far as you are ready to go. Pain is only inflicted if you want it."

Her shoulders relaxed. "Why would I want it?"

"Once you begin this journey you'll need more. Your body will crave the point where pleasure blends with pain."

She covered a groan and cleared her throat, which didn't help his growing erection straining against his fly. He took a deep breath and pulled the blindfold from her eyes. "You can let go now."

She hesitated, dropped her arm from the post and turned around. "That's it?"

"That's the abbreviated lesson. Isn't that what

you're looking for? Information?"

Her gaze lowered. "I guess so."

He moved to the cabinet and felt her eyes on him as he returned the blindfold and flogger and closed the doors. "Benjamin made breakfast. I would stay away from the toast, though." He turned and headed to the door as his heart jackhammered a hole in his chest.

"Walker?"

He stopped short but didn't turn around.

"What if I want more?"

"Is that a question or a statement?"

"I want more." Soft footfalls sounded behind him.

Walker turned and locked eyes with Stacia, and she closed the space between them. Her palms flattened on his chest and moved to his shoulders. Her body melded to his. He knew she could feel his rock-hard erection as she stepped closer and raised her face to his, never breaking eye contact.

He encircled his palms around her waist, swiveled, and backed her against the wall. Her breath was hot on his lips. "I don't think so, Princess. It's too soon."

She squared her shoulders. "I know what I want. This place makes me feel complete. It's like a piece of me was missing and I didn't realize what until now. Show me what I've been missing, Walker."

He grabbed a chunk of her hair, wrapped it around his fist and pulled down. The flesh of her throat contracted as she swallowed, but she wouldn't look away. "This isn't a game, Princess."

"I'm aware of that," she whispered.

He loosened his grip. "You don't know what you're getting yourself into."

"Maybe not. But if I don't find out, I'll never know. This just seems right to me, and I'm not sure why.

It's like I've been lost and just finding my way toward something familiar, even though everything here is so foreign." She dropped her gaze to the floor. "That probably makes no sense to you."

He hooked his index finger under her chin and captured her stare. "It makes sense. I get it, but I'm not convinced you're ready." He wanted nothing more than to give her what she asked. He'd never met anyone so receptive, but he had to be sure she was ready to be pushed to the limits of her breaking point. She needed to trust him. "How about we get out of here for a while?"

She furrowed her brows. "Out of the room?"

"Out of the house. Grab a pair of boots and a jacket and meet me downstairs in ten minutes. We're going for a ride."

Chapter Ten

He was screwed.

He should've already made a deal with Carlo and sent her home. It would've been the wise move. But the desire in her eyes kicked his heart into high gear, shooting sparks of electricity flowing through his veins. Dealing with Stacia was like playing with fire. Someone was going to be burned, but he wasn't about to let her go. Not yet. Not without giving her a taste of what she craved. Even though he'd never met anyone like her, he knew the inevitable would happen. He'd cast her off like he did the rest.

The fact didn't make him proud. It was just that. A fact. Walker wasn't capable of traditional relationships. They weren't in his DNA. He had figured that out many years ago. He'd tried to date women and made attempts at the doting boyfriend drill, but as soon as they pressed him to feel something he was incapable of feeling, he'd shown them who he was and what he wanted. The experience sent each one of them scrambling for the door. He'd given up on relationships and used private clubs to satisfy his itch, but he soon tired of staring into the empty eyes of women who turned to the clubs to help replace things lacking in their life. He wasn't interested in dealing with issues. He wanted a partner with his strength and one that wouldn't break. One who craved what he could offer. He wouldn't accept anything less. The problem was he wasn't convinced she existed.

Stacia could be his match, but she was too much of a challenge. Too independent. Too everything. She'd make his life a living hell, and that fact made long dead pieces of him come to life. It also scared the shit out of him, but that was the least of his problems. He was also aware that anyone connected to him would be a target. She could've been killed because of him, and he'd go to all costs before he'd allow that to happen again, even if it meant losing her forever, which would happen anyway. It was a matter of when, not if. His thoughts turned to her fascination with domination and submission. He knew she thirsted for it the moment he saw her face during the traffic reporting spots he had Benjamin pull when she appeared on their radar with the ongoing turf war with the Cardinelli family. Her eyes drew him in. After digging into her past and especially her computer viewing history, he knew what she craved. He also knew she needed it almost as much as she needed to breathe. Once she sampled the lifestyle everything would fall into place. His struggle would be giving her up after he possessed every part of her body and soul. But he would do it because he'd rather give himself to the Cardinellis than risk her safety.

"You know what you're doing?" Benjamin's question brought him back to the present.

He looked up and almost forgot he was pacing the kitchen floor. His mind was a million miles away.

Walker huffed and ran his hand through his hair. "No, I don't, Benjamin. For once in my life I don't know what the fuck I'm doing."

"Glad to see you're human. I often wonder," Benjamin said.

Walker pulled on his leather jacket. "Work the deal with Carlo while I'm gone. The faster we get this wrapped up the sooner we get on with our lives," he said, leaving through the back door. He strode across the patio to the garage and punched the security code into the keypad, suddenly glad he had his bike sent to New Orleans early. He stepped into the garage and pulled the dust cloth off one of his prize possessions.

A few minutes later footsteps sounded from behind. "Vintage Harley Panhead. Impressive." Stacia's voice echoed in the mostly empty garage. "'55?"

He folded the cloth, placing it on the shelf next to the helmets, before turning around. "'56. You have a good eye. Where'd you learn about bikes?"

"Ex-boyfriend. He was into old Harleys. He'd buy junkers and fix them up. He didn't have much money, so most of our dates were at salvage yards and chop shops. He'd pick me up on Weezy. It drove my father crazy."

"Weezy?"

She laughed. "That's what Jim named his bike. I swear I think he loved that thing more than me. He'd shit if he ever saw this. Bet you paid big bucks for it. You can't find original '56 Panheads anymore."

Walker huffed a sarcastic chuckle. "You think that's my answer to everything. Money."

"Isn't it? Money seems important to you."

He shrugged. "There's something more important. Pride. Pride in the work you do, pride in the people who share your goals, pride is what makes it worthwhile. Money is nice to have, don't get me wrong. But it's inconsequential without pride." He admired the bike's custom paintjob. "I rebuilt this bike. Took me five years."

She nodded. "You are full of surprises."

"That's my line," he chuckled. "Jim sounds like a good guy. Why aren't you still with him?"

"We decided to end things when I got the job at KCLA rather than try a long-distance relationship. He said LA might as well be Australia. He wasn't about to leave Cleveland, and he didn't want to hold me back from my dreams." Her fingers trailed along the seat. "What about you? You must have a girl in every city. Or are you more of a love 'em and leave 'em type?"

Walker picked up the spare helmet from the shelf and tossed it to Stacia. "Neither. Ready to go for a ride?"

"There you go, deflecting my questions again. It's a good thing I'm dying to see what this baby can do." She winked before putting her helmet on.

He slid the helmet over his head and straddled the bike. A rare sense of peace washed over his body as he jumped the pedal bringing his bike to life. Stacia slipped her leg over the seat behind him.

He turned his head. "Hold on," he said and revved the motor as she grabbed either side of his waist. They turned onto Prytania Road, leaving the mansion behind.

The wind licking at his cheeks reminded him how much he missed riding. He used to take his bike out practically every day, but life and Platinum blended into one entity and with it sucked all his time. He took a hard turn and her arms wrapped tighter around his waist, her hands linked together low on his abdomen. He fought the instinct to lay his palm over her hand, sending a silent message that she was safe. The action would wedge a splinter further into his already cracked exterior. He tried to deny she was inching her way under his skin, but it was getting harder, especially while her soft and warm parts pressed against the flesh of his back.

Walker revved the motor and made a sharp turn onto Tchoupitoulas Street, one of his favorite roads in New Orleans with the Mississippi River to one side and old warehouses on the other. Most of the buildings were gutted and turned into high-end condos, but the façades remained largely untouched. He slowed and came to a stop at the curb. He waited for Stacia to get off the bike before swinging his leg over and chaining it to a post.

"We going somewhere?" she asked scanning the

surroundings.

"A walk. You okay with that?"

"Yeah. It's just a strange choice. I mean, for New Orleans."

"Did you expect a stroll through art studios or voodoo shops? We're not on vacation, Princess."

"I never confuse being kidnapped and held against my will as a vacation. Jeez, why are you so f—" She paused and bit her lower lip. "…moody?" She lifted her index finger. "And I didn't hold back the f-bomb because *you* don't like it. I'm trying to cut down." She knocked him on the shoulder as he lifted an eyebrow. "You're an asshole, you know?"

Walker nodded. "You're not the first one to make that observation." He tipped his head to the left, and she fell into step next to him. "I like it here because it's not a tourist spot. But it's typical New Orleans. Old buildings are shells to a new generation of people and technology. Most of them are made up of condos."

Her gaze climbed the façade of an old warehouse. "High-priced condos, I'm sure. It's not much different from the Prytania Road house. Everything old becomes new again."

"I guess so. I come down here early in the morning for a run sometimes. Just me and the river. It's a great place to clear your head."

"Is that what we're doing here? Clearing our heads?"

His gaze tipped to her profile as they walked side by side. "Maybe. Sometimes a change of scenery helps you make the right decision. You asked me about my past relationships."

She turned toward him. "Ah, so you do actually listen to me."

He smiled. "I see and hear everything."

"I believe that. You even hear stuff you're not supposed to," she said with a grin.

Walker continued. "I've never had a real relationship. At least not what you'd consider a traditional one."

"Maybe you should rethink the whole asshole strategy."

He grunted a response.

"But that's not it, is it? Because I have friends who are madly in love with asshole men. There's more to it, and I think I know what it is."

"Give it your best shot," he said with equal parts curiosity and dread.

"You've never had a lasting relationship with a woman, not because you don't do relationships but because you haven't found the right person. Your ideal partner must keep up with you on every level of your life. Your life is your business, so she'd have to not only be okay with what you do, she needs to live it, too. She needs to be even stronger than you emotionally to deal with your moods. And most importantly, she needs to be compatible with you on a physical level. She needs to crave the journey you offer."

He continued walking in silence.

"I'm right, aren't I?"

"Is that important to you? To be right?" he asked. She was, in fact, spot on.

"Why do you answer every question with a question?"

"You just did it."

She stopped and faced the river. "I take pride in being right. It comes from being raised by a perfectionist. What's your excuse?"

"Why don't you tell me since you seem to know me so well."

Stacia tapped her chin and hummed. "Okay. The reason why you're a driven but reclusive control freak—"

"That's harsh."

"It's the truth," she said before biting her bottom lip in thought. "This is just a guess. The reason is because you were orphaned and grew up poor and alone. You're driven by making sure you have everything you never had when you were young."

"Sorry to tell you but that theory couldn't be further from the truth. My father was in the CIA. We lived all over the world, moving every few months. At fifteen my mother sent me to boarding school in the States so that I'd have some degree of consistency."

Stacia laughed. "That would've been my second guess. Did you mind being so far from your family?"

Walker rested his arm on the fence. "Not after I got used to it. Some of my classmates practically became family, Benjamin for example."

"You went to school with Benjamin?"

"I was a couple years ahead of him."

"Interesting. What made him want to work for you?"

"We didn't know each other really well in school. A bunch of guys and I wanted to play a prank for graduation so we broke into the auditorium and moved all of the statues from the grounds inside and put them on the stage dressed in bikinis."

Stacia laughed. "No."

"We were young and stupid. There wasn't much they could do about the seniors since we were graduating, but Benjamin dropped his school ID at the scene and they threatened him with expulsion. I took the rap for him and told them I took his ID."

"That was good of you."

Walker shrugged. "It was the right thing to do. We kept in touch after graduation, and he's started working with me after college."

"What about your dad? Did he want you to follow in his footsteps and join the CIA?"

"He tried and I considered it for a second, but I'm not good at taking orders."

"No! You?" Stacia said and bumped his hip.

He jerked his head toward the street. "Ready to head back?"

"You ask like I have a choice." They started back in the direction of his parked bike. "What was this all about anyway? We could've had the same conversation at the house. Not that I'm complaining."

"I want you to be sure of what you're agreeing to with me, Stacia. And I want you to realize that you can't change me. Others have tried and failed."

"Why would I want to change you? I kinda like you the way you are. Even if you are a brooding asshole." She squeezed his forearm. "Seriously though, I know what I'm getting myself into. And I also know it's not a forever thing. When this nightmare is over, I'll go back home and you'll be a distant memory. Don't worry about me, I'm a big girl."

He searched her eyes. "Man, that was harsh."

She raised her brows. "But true."

"Good to know because it may happen sooner than later. We found Jake. Benjamin's negotiating a deal with Carlo as we speak. You'll be able to go back to your life and never have to worry about Jake or the Cardinellis or me again. This whole thing will seem like a crazy dream in a few days."

The words sank in and rooted deep in his belly.

"Everything is falling into place then," she said quietly. They walked in silence and stopped when they reached his motorcycle. Her gaze cast down for a moment before she gave him a side-eyed look. "You'll miss me when I'm gone."

"Miss keeping you safe from a notorious crime boss? Doubt it." He handed her a helmet. But he wasn't ready to let her go. Not yet.

Chapter Eleven

The Walker who'd opened up and given her a small taste retreated into his tough exterior with every passing mile. Even his skin felt cold through his jacket as they raced back to Prytania Road. By the time they pulled into the garage, his hard shell was firmly in place. He strode across the patio and held the door open where she spotted Benjamin seated at the kitchen counter.

"Is it done?" Walker barked.

"Carlo's in agreement with the deal. Stacia can return home safely anytime she chooses," Benjamin answered.

"Good." Walker nodded and turned to Stacia. "Looks like you have a decision to make. Benjamin will go over some information with you. Think hard about what he tells you. If you still want this, meet me in the Tower Room at nine."

How could one man be almost human one moment and such a dick the next? "How romantic."

He moved closer and cupped her cheek into his palm. "I don't do romance, Princess." He dropped his hand, and she didn't realize how much heat he held in his palm until it was gone. He strode through the back door. Moments later, Stacia's ears perked from the sound of a motor outside and her gaze turned to the window as the familiar black-clad form on a motorcycle disappeared from the property. Footsteps drew her attention from the window as Benjamin appeared. "Why does he just disappear like that?"

Benjamin waved his hand toward the stool at the kitchen counter gesturing for Stacia to sit. "I don't know. I'm not sure if he does either," Benjamin said, pouring a cup of coffee and handing it to Stacia.

The warmth grounded her thoughts that were

flying in every direction. "Thank you," she said wrapping her hands around the mug. "Does he always up and leave when he's not happy? Seems childish to me," she muttered.

"I think Walker removes himself from situations to benefit those around him. What you've seen is nothing. I've been around him when he's fired up. You don't want to see that."

"I'm a big girl. I don't need protecting."

"Really?"

She noticed his half smile and was happy for the bit of humor that cut through the tension. "I guess that was pretty stupid considering you two just saved my life." Her cheeks warmed in embarrassment.

"Walker told you we found Jake. While you were gone, I ironed out an agreement to ensure your protection. You're safe and free to go if you'd like."

Her mind raced to the conversation with Walker in the Tower Room. This was her out if she chose to take it. Her gaze moved to the window. "Is he always this intense?"

Benjamin chuckled. "Walker runs on two speeds: Intense and Highly Intense."

She turned to Benjamin. "How does he do it? How do *you* do it?"

"Walker may be intense, but you'll never know anyone as loyal. I'd step in front of a bullet for him, and I know he'd do the same for me. Once you're in Walker's inner circle, you're there for life." Benjamin laid both palms on the counter. "What's your decision, Stacia? I can have the jet ready to take you home in an hour. Or you can choose to stay the evening."

"I'm staying."

"I take that as a confirmation of your attendance at your meeting with Walker later this evening."

She took a sip of the steaming black coffee. "You make it sound so formal."

"It's my job to make you aware of what you're getting into."

"I think I know what I'm getting myself into."

His eyes locked with hers. "You have no idea what you're getting into. What you've seen in your research is not what it will be like with Walker. His intensity follows him in every aspect of his life. It will be like nothing you've experienced."

Her stomach performed perfect ten-point flip, and the heat simmering deep in her belly traveled south.

"Also, I've seen women challenge themselves to change him. They couldn't, and you won't either. If you're looking to play games, he's not interested. If you're looking for flowers and chocolates, he's not your guy."

"Man, Benjamin. No rose-colored glasses for you. You're one of those glass half empty people, aren't you?"

"This isn't a joke, Stacia."

"You two keep reminding me of that. I know it's not a joke, and I'm up to it. And you can tell your employer he'd better not fall in love with me because I'm not interested either."

Benjamin nodded. "I'll relay the message. Now, let's go over Walker's explicit instructions in which you should not deviate unless agreed upon by both parties in advance."

She was reminded of his matter-of-fact tone while he went over the NDA on the plane. "You're not going to whip out another contract for me to sign, are you Benjamin?"

"No contract. Walker wants things the way he expects them. This is no different. Are you ready to hear his instructions?"

"You mean demands?"

Benjamin cleared his throat and rested both hands on the counter. "No one is forcing you to do this. I can make a call and have the jet ready to take you home within the hour. Just say the word. But if this is what you want, you have to do it by Walker's rules."

Part of her wanted to leave. Who the hell was he to make demands on her actions and body? But overwhelming desire flooded her soul with every heartbeat. She took a deep breath. "I'm listening."

Chapter Twelve

Stacia's heels sank into plush carpet as she stepped into the Tower Room illuminated only by the flaming logs in the fireplace and lit candelabras placed on either side of the bed. She rolled her shoulders, and the leather straps of the corset softened from the heat of her skin and stroked her flesh. She'd wanted to wear it the moment she spotted it in the closet. Walker must've seen her admire it because it was hanging on the mirror in her bedroom along with a pair of lace panties and black Louboutin stilettos. She wasn't sure if Benjamin, Walker, or someone else picked out the clothes that appeared in the house upon her arrival. Whoever it was had amazing taste. She slowly circled the perimeter of the room once and then again. She knew he was watching. His gaze burned through her body.

Her eyes steadied on the fire as she stood in front of the mantel when the click of the door knob sounded followed by the soft close of the door. "Were my instructions unclear?"

"They were very clear," she said without moving her gaze.

"But you chose to ignore them?"

"I chose to ignore some of them." She turned, and her heart fluttered when she laid eyes on Walker. Judging by his choice of leather corset for her, she wondered if he'd also be in leather. During her research, she'd seen pictured of men dressed in outrageous outfits including leather pants, jackets with zippers and buckles, and even hoods. She was relieved to see him barefoot in a pair of jeans and a fitted t-shirt. "As you can see, I'm wearing the ensemble you picked out."

"*You* picked it out," he corrected. "What happened to the rest of the instructions?"

"I know you wanted to find me in a submissive position of your choice, but I have questions that need answers before I choose to lay my body down for you," she said, the words tumbling from her mouth before she lost her nerve.

"Benjamin said you didn't have any questions."

"My questions aren't for Benjamin. They're for you."

He hesitated before nodding and moving to one of the large armchairs next to the fireplace. "Fair enough. Take a seat." He waited until she sat in the twin chair beside his. "What's on your mind?"

"First. This corset."

"You don't like it?"

"I like it. Very much. What I don't like is the reason why this and other article of clothes like it were in the closet waiting or me or … someone else."

"They are all for you, no one else. You think it was forward of me to assume you'd want them. And I agree."

"You do?"

He nodded. "One of Benjamin's jobs is to ensure my guests have everything they want during their stay. He took it upon himself to order these things for you."

"You didn't know anything about them?"

"Not until you opened the closet. Do you have another question?"

"How many women have you taken up here?"

"Only you."

She lifted her brows.

"For this to work you have to put your trust in me. You're the only woman who has been a guest in this room and also in this house, as a matter of fact."

Stacia's gaze traveled to his eyes, and she nodded. "I believe you."

"There's something else inside your head that's holding you back. What is it?"

He was right. It had troubled her all day. "Why'd you leave today? Why was it Benjamin who went through the details like it was some sort of impersonal business agreement?"

"For you. In case you wanted to back out it would've been easier to tell Benjamin than me."

"That's not true, and frankly it's taking the coward's way out. If I changed my mind, I'd have no problem telling you. But on the flip side, if you want something from me, I expect *you* to tell me. Not Benjamin. Deal?"

"Deal." He narrowed his eyes. "Is there anything else?"

"No."

"Good. Before we start, let's talk safewords. I prefer using the colors of a stoplight. I'll check in with you a lot, especially since it's your first time. If everything is good your answer is green. If you're starting to feel uncomfortable about what I'm doing, you'll answer yellow. If you want to stop you say red. You can say it at any time, not only when I ask."

"Got it. Benjamin went through this with me. We also talked about hard limits. Again, it was a conversation I would've rather had with you."

"Point taken and I'm glad you told me. Sometimes it's hard for me to switch from business mode." He shrugged. "The most important thing to remember is it may seem like the dominant one has all the power in a scene, but it's quite the opposite. You are the one with the power. You guide what happens in here. It's your journey."

"How does that make you feel?"

Fire blazed in his eyes. "It's not about me,

Princess. Kneel on the bed facing the wall."

His first order made her body hum, but she needed something first. "Before we start, may I ask you for something?"

"I should deny you, but I'm curious. What is it?"

Her gaze moved from his eyes to his lips. "A kiss."

"I don't do that." The words fell from his lips, but his gaze held something else entirely.

"Benjamin told me that, too, but I didn't believe him and it's something I need."

"Why?"

"Because a kiss will connect us. It'll break the ice. Tear down barriers." Her voice lowered. "It'll make me feel okay about laying myself raw and bare to you."

"You think a kiss will do all that?" He moved closer.

"I know it will."

"You don't know what you're getting yourself into."

"Try me."

Walker stepped in front of her. The heat radiated from his body as his palms captured her bare shoulders. "This won't change me, Princess."

"Why would I want to change you?"

"Most women do."

"I'm not most women."

"I'm acutely aware of that." His grip tightened on her shoulders. She lifted to the balls of her feet as his mouth crashed on hers with raw and unapologetic abandon. His tongue invaded her mouth, taking what he desired and sending a message loud and clear. It was a warning, and she wasn't backing down. He pulled away, and she touched her lips as she caught her breath.

"Satisfied?"

She locked his gaze. "I'm far from satisfied."

He shrugged off his shirt. The flames of the fireplace threw shadows along the dips and planes of his muscular flesh and highlighted the ink decorating his arms and torso. Her gaze washed over his chest and held on one design. It was familiar, but she couldn't place where she'd seen it.

"Problem?" he asked.

"Your tattoo. It looks familiar." She reached out, but he grabbed her wrist and her gaze whipped up to meet his blazing eyes.

"This isn't your rodeo, Princess. Stand at the foot of the bed."

Chapter Thirteen

She hesitated.

Stacia wasn't used to taking orders.

He studied her expression as her eyes locked on the tattoo decorating his chest. The one that reminded him of his purpose every morning when he caught its reflection in the bathroom mirror. Her eyes narrowed and flicked to his before returning to his ink.

"The bed. Now." Her comment about his tattoo churned in his head. The intricate design of a series of swords and shields inside a ring of snakes was exclusive to Platinum agents. There was no way she could've seen it before. Something similar, maybe. But the actual design? Impossible. He'd question her later. He had more immediate concerns, like damage control from that damn kiss. Why'd he agree to it? It was time to take back control. His gaze roamed her body.

She stood at the foot of the bed with her arms at her side and her head straight like someone about to go into battle. It wasn't what he had expected for a first-timer. She lacked the usual telltale nervous motions like hugging her arms, shifting from one foot to the other, or simple fidgeting. Her stance was alert. For someone so headstrong and defiant, her willingness to experience a scene with him was surprisingly complicated. Stacia's drive and tenacity matched his, but there was a piece of her that wanted to sacrifice control for her own pleasure. And that made her the sexiest woman he'd ever known. And the most dangerous.

He'd planned to take it easy on her, but given the kiss and her readiness, he decided to forego his initial strategy. He strode to the wood paneled wall on the far side of the room and pulled a latch built into the carved molding, releasing a hidden door. Wires hung from the top and sides of the interior for lighting that hadn't yet been installed. However, there was a piece of equipment inside that was sure to put her on edge. He felt around the dark compartment until his fingers grazed cool leather. He grabbed the item from the hook and a series of clinks sounded over the crackle of the fire. Carrying the equipment toward the bed, he allowed the four chains attached to the corners of leather to drag on the floor. Stacia turned her head toward the sound.

"I didn't tell you to turn around, Princess," he said.

Her head whipped back. "What is that?"

"You don't have permission to talk either." He moved to the side of the bed. Her eyes flicked to him then straight ahead. He dropped it on the bed and carefully stretched the chains toward each of the bed posts. He slowly moved to each corner and slid a link from each chain onto the recessed hooks in the post. Leaning his knee on the bed, he pushed his palms onto the harness. The warm crack of the leather sent electricity up his spine. He moved to the cabinet and wrapped his hand around a leather-bound riding crop. He felt her eyes on him and turned, catching her gaze for a fraction of a second before her gaze shifted ahead. He moved to the side of the bed and gripped the crop in his hand. With a quick flick of his wrist the implement sliced through the air and hit the mattress with a whack. "Kneel on the bed in front of the harness."

For once she didn't argue. Instead, she placed one knee on the bed and then the other with her arms at her side.

"Put your arms above your head and lean over."

She did what he asked. The cool clinking of the chains combined with the warm stretching of the leather harness. He reached behind the headboard, grabbing a cord that was attached to the frame. "Put your hands together." He pulled the cord until it was taut and wound it around her wrists a few times before he tied a knot. "Hey," he said pulling her gaze from her bound hands to his eyes. "You okay?"

She glanced at her hands again. "Yeah, but it's a whole lot different to experience it than to watch or read about it." A shiver ran over her body and goosebumps covered her arms.

He held her forearms in his palms and rubbed her skin. "Are you cold?" He'd seen new subs go into shock during their first time, and he wanted to make sure Stacia wasn't hiding her fear behind a strong front.

She shook her head. "I'm fine."

He trailed his hands over the cord and held her fingers loosely in his grasp. "Be sure you can twist your wrists."

She rotated her hands easily.

"Good. Tell me if it gets too tight." He gave her fingers a light squeeze and headed back to the cabinet for the next accessory. He reached to the back and pulled out a heavy metal bar with cuffs at either end.

Stacia's eyes widened. "What's that for?"

"Your feet."

"Holy shit," she muttered.

He cracked a smile. "I'm looking forward to cleaning up that mouth of yours," he said and dropped the bar on the edge of the mattress. He pulled her ankles further apart and rolled the bar into the space between her feet and buckled the straps around her ankles. His gaze followed the curve of her calf up to her creamy inner thigh to her round ass, covered only by the strip of her black lace thong. Her bare shoulder blades rose and fell faster as she tried to move her feet.

"Color, Princess?" he asked.

He noticed a hesitation, and she cleared her throat. "Still green. But…"

"Yes?"

"I can't move."

"That's the point of bondage. You're giving up control and giving in to trust."

"I get it, but I didn't know it'd be this hard to do."

He let her words hang above them like a cloud and waited to see if her nerves would get the best of her and she'd safeword out. He hoped she wouldn't because the vision in front of him was more beautiful than he'd ever imagined. His gaze swept over her body and lingered at the juncture between her legs. Even though her sex was partially covered by the thin piece of lace, he glimpsed the evidence of how turned on she was and they'd barely begun.

Walker moved to her side and leaned over so he was inches from her ear. "Nothing worthwhile is easy, Princess. I promised I'd help you fly. Trust me to do exactly that."

Stacia's shoulders softened, and she took a deep breath in silent answer to his request.

He made a final trip to the cabinet where he pulled a silk sash from a drawer and took from the hook the flogger they'd used earlier that day. He placed the flogger on the mattress and combed the fabric of the sash through his fingers, chasing the chill from the cool silk. Holding it between his thumbs and index fingers of both hands, he leaned onto the bed and placed it over her eyes. Stacia gasped as he tied it at the back of her head. "Do you know the purpose of the blindfold?"

"So I could focus on the tactile experience."

He was sure it was a line out of her research, but she'd soon make her own discovery.

"It's easier to let yourself go when there's

nothing to see." He was glad his own vision wasn't compromised because the view before him was more magnificent than he'd imagined. Her legs were spread in a way that raised her round ass like an invitation to be spanked. He trailed the end of the crop up her leg, over her ass, and along the seam of the corset. "How are you doing?"

"It feels like every nerve ending is standing at attention."

He smiled and traded the crop for the flogger. Again, he dragged it slowly over her body following the same line as the crop. However, when he reached her shoulders, he moved to the opposite side of the bed and continued his journey on the other side. He stopped when he got to her ass, fisted the flogger tight in his grasp, and lightly whipped it across her skin.

She called out, and the chains rattled as she squirmed in the harness. He flicked his wrist, and the dozen or so straps of the flogger thrashed over her skin with even more force. Stacia called out again louder.

"Color," he demanded.

"Green," Stacia bit out.

He took a step toward the foot of the bed and used a backhand motion to direct the next swing at the back of her left thigh above her knee. Stacia groaned, and the cord holding her hands scraped along the headboard. He sent an identical thrash over the inside of her right thigh. The muscles of her legs tightened as her breath grew ragged. She writhed in the harness and tried to hitch her ass higher, giving him more access. The lips of her sex were full and gleamed with arousal through the lace. He aimed his next swipe higher on her thigh so that some of the blades came within a whisper of her pussy. The bed creaked as she pulled at the cord again and clenched her teeth.

"Don't fight it. Breathe and slip into the wave like you're walking into the ocean. Let it take you, Princess," he said softly.

She loosened her fingers and let her arms relax.

"Good. Now take a deep breath and let it out slowly through your mouth."

She followed his directive, and he watched her body relax. Walker leaned one knee on the mattress and gave her four more lashes in quick succession to her thighs and ass but avoiding the lace strip of material. She moaned through the flogging and pled for more when he stopped. Strands of hair stuck to her forehead damp with perspiration.

"Please," she whispered.

His bare palm landed hard and heavy on her ass cheek. He rubbed the red mark that crept under his hand. He pulled a switchblade from his pocket, opened the knife, and ran the dull side along her hip. Her head quirked as he slid the cold metal along her flesh.

"What is that?"

"Do you trust me, Princess?"

He watched her neck as she swallowed hard. "Yes."

"What's your color?"

"Green. Still green," she said in a raspy voice.

He fisted the lace band at her hip, sliced it with a flash of the blade, and replicated the motion on the other side. The tattered thong fell to the mattress and the sweet scent of her sex combined with melted candle wax filled his senses. His cock pressed against the zipper of his jeans. He was within inches of burying himself into her slick, wet heat. But he wouldn't cross that line. He was already in too far. She arched her back, and he trailed two fingers along her gleaming folds before sliding them into her core. Fuck, she was wet and tight and perfect.

She groaned and rocked her body into his hand. He pulled his fingers out and traced them down to her clit. He lightly circled the hood as he pressed his denim-clad erection against her ass. Garbled words fell from her lips as she writhed in the harness. While circling her clit, he pushed two fingers of his other hand into her sex. Her muscles contracted once, and he pulled away.

"Fuck no!" she cried. "Don't stop."

He smirked. "I said you'd pay for your dirty mouth."

A sound of frustration ran through her lungs. He understood exactly what she was going through because hell if he wasn't feeling the same.

"You're not going to leave me like this?"

"Is that a statement or a question? Because if it's a statement, I sure as hell will."

"No. Please."

"Please what?"

"I want to come. Please?"

He leaned forward. His mouth was centimeters from her glistening folds. He parted his lips and blew a slow breath over her sex as he traced his fingers up her inner thigh.

"Oh God," she whispered.

He ran the tip of his tongue along her folds and copied the same movement around her clit with his fingers. Stacia bucked against the holster, but he kept his slow pace. "Walker, please," she cried, and her legs shook.

His mouth possessed her sex, and his fingers moved in the same rhythm as Stacia's release came hard. The chains rattled and leather holster stretched in rhythm with her screams as he coaxed every contraction from her body. His movements slowed along with her breath as she came down from her orgasm. But he was still keyed up tighter than a guitar. His cock strained along his zipper and begged for relief. One that would have to wait until he was alone in the shower he'd take after he'd put her to bed. He released the cuffs from her legs, rubbing each ankle between his palms. He moved to her hands and untied the cord from her wrists. He laced his fingers with hers and lightly massaged her hand and arm, then switching to the other. Finally, he pulled the sash from her eyes.

"Hi," she said with a coy smile.

He pulled a plush blanket from the cabinet and helped her out of the harness before laying the blanket around her shoulders.

"Thank you," she said.

He gathered her in his arms. "Don't try to talk right now. It takes a while to come down." He set her down on one of the winged armchairs next to the fire. "I'll be right back," he said and slipped into the front room. He returned with a warm cloth and a cup of tea. Walker handed her the steaming mug before hooking his thumb under her chin and guiding her head upward to meet his gaze. He wiped her forehead and cheeks with the corner of the cloth as she watched him intently. "How are you feeling?"

"I'm feeling so much but most of all refreshed and energized. Like a weight was lifted from my shoulders. One that I didn't know was there until this moment."

It was confirmation that she did indeed crave what he could provide. It was only the beginning. He wished he could show her the world he knew she desired. But he knew he couldn't.

She took a sip from her mug. "Looks like I'm doing far better than you are." Her gaze floated down his body to the bulge in his pants, which hadn't subsided.

He chuckled, slumped into the chair next to her, and watched the dying flames in the fireplace. "Don't worry about me, Princess."

She stood, placed her mug on the table between the two chairs and took a step forward so she stood in between his outstretched legs. The blanket slid from one of her shoulders as she lowered her knees to the floor. Her fingers trailed up his legs, and she cupped her palm over the bulge in his pants, sending even more heat to the fire burning low in his belly.

"Stacia. No."

She released the button of his pants and pinched the zipper between her thumb and finger. "No isn't a safeword. If you really want me to stop you have to say red." Her gaze moved from below his waist to meet his eyes.

His heart kicked his chest as he pierced her with a stare. "This isn't a game."

"I'm aware of that." The zipper grazed his erection as it lowered. "You're rough." She reached inside and ran her nails along the length of his shaft. "You're raw." She yanked his pants down and wrapped her palm around his girth. "And you're hard. So very hard."

"Fuck," he hissed as she took him completely into her mouth, wet and hot. There was no teasing with shy licks or testing her ability to handle his size. He bucked as the underside of his cock slid along her tongue and hit the back of her throat. He fisted a chunk of her hair and pulled. A ragged groan expelled from his throat as he watched her hollowed cheeks and glistening lips rise from his dick. "Look at me," he commanded.

Her lids fluttered before lifting to his gaze. Golden eyes stared back filled with surrender. He tightened his grasp and pumped her head along his length as she fought to keep eye contact. He widened his thighs as she took his balls into her palm. Loosening his grip on her hair, he held her face between his hands and bent forward, slowing the rhythm on his cock as he teetered on the edge of his climax. He gritted his teeth, holding on as long as he could.

"I'm close," he bit out, giving her a chance to finish with her hand. She shook her head and her cheeks hollowed further. She not only took every inch of him, she was going to swallow his seed, too. There was no turning back. Every expletive he knew flew from his mouth as his hands raked through her hair, pumping her swollen lips over his aching cock until he shot hot cum against the back of her throat. She closed her eyes for a moment and tears fell to her cheeks when she opened them again. He released his fingers from her tangled hair and leaned back as his cock pulsed into her mouth. She rested her head in his lap, and he lazily stroked her hair as they caught their breath.

"Hey." He barely recognized his husky voice.

She hitched her elbow on his thigh and rested her head on her hand. Her hair stuck up in every direction. Tears stained her cheeks, and her lips were red and swollen. She was the most beautiful thing he'd ever seen. A sharp pain pierced his chest knowing he'd soon say goodbye to Stacia forever.

Chapter Fourteen

Walker's bad decisions bit him in the balls the next morning.

"I thought it was done." His fist landed with a thud on the counter.

"It was until Carlo threw the Miami resort into the deal. It's his last request," Benjamin answered. "You agree and the deal is done."

Walker paced the kitchen and stopped at the window overlooking the garden lit in the warm glow of the rising sun. "He wants it as a holding place for the girls he's smuggling from Mexico before he places them in other clubs. I can't do it."

Benjamin peered over his laptop from his place at the kitchen's island. "If you don't he'll find another place. At least we know this one. You know the floorplan, and we can install surveillance inside before we hand it over. It can help the overall mission and you can send Stacia home."

That was the plan. In fact, the pilot was readying the jet to shuttle her back to LA later that day. All that was left to do was say goodbye and she'd be out of his life forever. Benjamin's laptop chimed.

"Another message from Carlo." Benjamin tapped the keyboard. "He said you have five minutes to make a decision or he has no choice but to take something from you that can't be replaced."

"What the hell are you talking about, Benjamin?" Walker snapped. There was nothing in Walker's life that couldn't be replaced. It was a perk of having money, and lots of it.

Benjamin waved his hand at the screen. "Just delivering the message." Another chime sounded. "Hold on. There's more." He tapped his keyboard again. "You need to see this."

Walker rounded the island and his gaze hit the screen. One image after another of Stacia and him walking along the river downloaded onto the monitor. A knot curled up like a fist in his throat. As a new message appeared.

We seemed to have found your weakness, Walker. Consider it a gift that we spared her life twice now. I assure you it won't happen again.

"We took every precaution to keep our location private. How'd he find us?" The Prytania house wasn't part of Platinum's real estate holdings. His gaze trailed along the images. One made him hold his breath. He was leaning on the fence staring into the water. At the time, he'd thought she was doing the same, but the camera caught Stacia staring at his face. Walker swiveled the laptop toward him and clicked on the photo enlarging it to full screen. Trust hung heavy in her eyes, but something else was there, too. He'd witnessed it in her gaze last night in the Tower Room. She was falling in love with him, and it almost got her killed. "I let her down," he said, sliding the laptop back to Benjamin.

"There was no way of knowing they had our location. Besides, she's safe. She's with us." Benjamin closed the laptop. "What are you going to do, Walker?"

Carlo had him at the edge of a cliff. If he stepped one way he'd risk Stacia's life, but if he chose the other option, it would mean opening the door for Carlo's human trafficking ring, potentially impacting hundreds of innocent girls. He rubbed his eyes with the heels of his palms.

"I need to think." He jerked his head toward the stairs. "She'll be up soon. Don't let her go outside. Not even on the patio." He strode into the hallway between the kitchen and staff quarters and ran his hand over the wood molding releasing a latch and revealing a hidden door. Walker tightened his fists as he descended the stairs. He needed to punch something. The door closed with a soft thud as recessed lights illuminated his second favorite, but most important, floor of the Prytania house. Since New Orleans was below sea level, most homes weren't built with a basement, but this one was a necessary enhancement. Housing a state-of-the-art gym, wine cellar, and a control room that doubled as an emergency safe room, the underground level was the heart of the house.

Walker shucked his shirt, balled it up, and threw it in the corner while he kicked off his shoes and slipped on a pair of boxing gloves that hung from a hook on the wall of his gym next to a set of free weights. He strode to the leather punching bag hanging from the ceiling. The images of Stacia's photos scrolling on the screen stabbed him in the gut. With one command from Carlo, the asshole behind the camera could've replaced it with a gun. Walker failed to keep her safe because he'd crossed the line and gotten too close. He tried to fool himself by pretending it was for her, but it was just as much for him. From the moment he touched her, a craving crept up his spine and grabbed hold of his soul. Walker pummeled the bag with a succession of punches. The chain clanked and echoed through the quiet room as the bag strained against his assault. Sweat dripped from his forehead, stinging his eyes, and his tight muscles burned. Stacia could not be put at risk again. He wouldn't allow it.

Walker pulled the gloves off and chucked them into the corner as he sucked cool air into his lungs with his ragged breath. His gaze caught the mirror, landing on the circular tattoo that Stacia recognized the night before. He stepped toward the mirror and studied the design. He'd made a vow to protect on the day it was permanently inked on his chest ten years ago. The tattoo signified who he was and what he had become. The design depicted a detailed ring of snakes drawing the eye to the center of swords resting over his heart. There were only a handful of men with the same design, all of them Platinum agents. Stacia had to be mistaken. It was impossible for her to have seen it before, or was he missing something?

Walker shook his head. Stacia was a reporter and a damn good one. She had an eye for detail. She must've seen it before, and he needed to know where. He strode into the safe room and poked a button on the control panel. "Is she up?"

"She's up."

"Send her down."

A quiet pause filled the space. "We agreed to keep that level classified," Benjamin said in a hushed voice.

He took a deep breath. Yet again all rules and protocol flew out the window when it came to Stacia. "Send her down, Benjamin."

He stepped back into the gym as the door clicked and hesitant footsteps sounded from behind. "Holy shit, I feel like I'm walking into the Batcave. Alfred up there had his panties in a bunch about me coming down here."

Walker chuckled. "You a Batman fan, too?"

"Only of the cheesy sixties series. Christian Bale has nothing on Adam West," she said scanning the underground level. "Care to show me around, Bruce Wayne?"

He lifted his hands. "Gym, obviously. Over there is the heart of the house. All of the surveillance and security controls run through the panel."

"May I?" She pointed to the room.

He nodded and followed her inside.

"Looks like a vault," she said, examining the thick steel door.

"It doubles as a safe room. There are sleeping quarters and provisions for emergencies."

She studied the monitors, keypads, and buttons. "You're not fucking around."

He raised his eyebrows.

"I said I'd cut down on the f-bombs, not eliminate them. What else is down here?"

"Just a wine cellar."

"Because you can't be stuck in a safe room without a great vintage Boudreaux. You are an interesting man, Walker." Her gaze trailed unapologetically down his body, pausing on his bare chest. "Why did you send me down here?"

"Last night," he began, but his thoughts shifted to the Tower Room, stirring his dick in the process.

"Last night," she repeated. Her throat worked a swallow, and she licked her lips.

He cleared his throat and strode past her, hiding the growing bulge in his jeans. She followed him out of the safe room.

"You said you recognized my tattoo." He stood in front of the mirror, his gaze following her reflection as she walked to his side.

"I do." Their eyes met in the mirror.

"From where?"

"Why?"

"I need to know, Stacia."

"Hmm, let me take a closer look." She moved forward, turned to face him, and leaned her back against the mirror. Her finger lightly traced the outside border over his chest, sending heat directly to his cock. His hands ached to tease her nipples pebbling through the light fabric of her shirt. Her index finger trailed to the center of the tattoo and slowly continued downward toward the button of his jeans.

Encircling her wrist, he pulled her hand away and stepped closer, the heat of her body blanketing his chest. It was like an invisible rope pulling him in. "Damn it, Princess," he bit out.

"Why are you trying so hard to fight it?" she whispered softly against his mouth.

His thoughts slowed and his brain fogged as he inhaled her intoxicating scent. A thread of restraint kept him from tearing off her clothes and sinking into her core his cock, straining at the zipper of his jeans. But as quickly as he succumbed, he shook the fog from his head. Getting too close was how he ended up in this mess. He wouldn't allow it to happen again. His task was to protect Stacia and take down the Cardinellis. Neither could be accomplished with his brain in a fuck fog. He stepped back and dragged his hand over his face. "It's important. If you've seen this tattoo on someone else I need to know."

"My father has the same one on his chest."

"Your father? That's not possible." His mind raced. There was only one of his agents who could be the age of Stacia's father.

She tilted her head, and her eyes tipped to his chest again. "I'm pretty sure, but it's not like I saw it much. General Howell has always been a buttoned-up kind of man. He never walked around without a shirt so I'm not even sure how long he's had it, but I noticed it last time I visited. I took him for a stress test and walked in while he was putting his shirt back on. I asked him about it, and he quickly buttoned his shirt and changed the subject. But I remembered it because it was so unique. It took me a while to place where I saw it before when I saw yours, but I'm sure it's the same as his. I remember the ring of snakes and swords pointing to the center. What does it mean?"

Damn it. Why didn't he figure out the connection before? "It means your father is the link between you and me, and Carlo discovered it. It's why he targeted you."

"What do you mean he's the link?" she asked.

"It means your father is a Platinum agent."

"My father? Impossible."

"No?" He jerked his head toward the safe room and strode to the panel and tapped a button. "Benjamin, come down here please."

Walker poked another button a monitor illuminated as a keyboard lowered from a panel.

"What's going on?" Benjamin asked, appearing at Walker's side.

"Get Nighthawk on this thing," Walker ordered.

Benjamin tipped his head toward Stacia. "Nighthawk is classified. All our agents are."

"We're making an exception in this case."

Benjamin rolled a stool to the desk. "Seems we're making a lot of those lately," he muttered as he tapped on the keyboard.

"Walker." A strong voice boomed from the monitor. Walker studied the man's face. There was little resemblance between the man he knew only as Nighthawk and Stacia. Her looks must've come from her mother. Walker had known Nighthawk since Platinum's inception. As Nighthawk was Platinum's military advisor, Walker never knew his true identity, only that he was retired from the armed forces. Walker respected Nighthawk's request to remain anonymous and use a code name due to his past classified status in the military.

"Nighthawk, sir," Walker began.

"Dad?" Stacia said, staring at the screen.

"Stacia? What are you—Walker, what's going

on? What are you doing with my daughter?"

"Protecting her sir." He pinched the bridge of his nose between his thumb and index finger. If the man only knew what else he was doing with his daughter. "The Cardinellis must've figured out the connection. They lured her to Las Vegas with a story, and we believe they were going to kidnap her. We intercepted, and she's been under our watch since then."

"Why is this the first I'm hearing about this? Stacia, you told me you were on assignment," Nighthawk barked. His eyes bounced from one side of the monitor to the other.

"I was. At least I thought I was," Stacia answered. "He always makes me feel like I'm five years old," she whispered.

"I heard that, Stacia. What's your location? I'm coming to get you and bring you home."

"It's too dangerous. Carlo used Stacia to get to us. We just figured it out, which is why we didn't contact you earlier. She's safer here with me. I'm going to send backup to your location."

"No need, Walker. I can take care of myself. Does Cardinelli know where she is?"

"No," Walker lied, detecting Benjamin's glare in his direction. "We're in final negotiations with Carlo, which will include the guarantee of Stacia's safety."

Nighthawk rubbed his temple. The lines in his face appeared more pronounced. "Keep me updated and keep her safe, Walker."

"Dad." Stacia's eyes welled up. "I'm sorry. I should've talked to you about the assignment. I thought—"

"You didn't think, Stacia." Nighthawk's eyes cast down, and the monitor went dark as he ended the connection.

"Son of a bitch," she said, swiping a tear from her cheek. "This is so typical."

"He's upset. It's understandable," Walker said.

Stacia raised her palm. "Don't try to explain General Howell to me. I know him better than you." She shrugged. "Maybe that's not even true. You two are some sort of vigilante partners. I had no idea he was working as an agent. I thought he was retired and home tending his garden. I don't know what to think. I'm going upstairs. This is all a lot to take in for one morning."

Walker and Benjamin were silent until they heard Stacia's footsteps on the floor above. "Why didn't you tell him?" Benjamin asked.

"Tell him what?"

"You know what. The pictures? Carlo knowing our location?"

"It's better he doesn't know. If he knew, he'd come and there's too much risk in that. As long as she's in this house with us, she's better protected than anywhere else. This is all going to be over soon."

"I don't agree, Walker. That's his daughter. He should know. I think you don't want to admit you made a mistake."

He wished for that moment Benjamin didn't know him so well. "The reason I didn't tell him is to protect her."

"Sounds like you're protecting yourself. It's not like you. She's getting under your skin and clouding your judgment."

"Stop worrying about my judgment and focus on Carlo agreeing to our terms so we can all move on with our lives."

It was easier said than done.

Chapter Fifteen

She's getting under your skin and clouding your judgment. Benjamin's words haunted Walker mostly because they were true. Stacia had taken root under his skin, and the result could put them all in danger. He had no choice but to avoid her as much as possible until they finished negotiations with Carlo, which had stalled.

The third day without hearing from the Cardinellis came and went. He did the best he could to avoid interacting with Stacia. He spent most of his time at the control panel in the safe room monitoring online mob chatter and waiting for communication from Carlo.

The next morning Stacia headed him off in the hall before he opened the latch to the basement stairs. "I'm crawling the walls here, Walker. Let's take a ride to get a beignet or something."

Walker narrowed his eyes. He didn't miss the hurt that passed over hers, making him feel like an ass for the position he'd put them both in. "We can't risk it," he said, trying to move past her.

Stacia stepped in his way preventing him from passing. "You said yourself he doesn't know where we are. I don't see the harm in getting out for an hour."

"You want to go outside? The patio is right out there." He hitched his thumb over his shoulder.

"Yeah and I can't even go out there by myself." Stacia folded her arms. "I need to join the land of the living. Walk among people. I need to get out of here for a while. I'm going crazy in here with the two of you."

Walker leaned back in his chair. "My answer is the same as it was yesterday and the day before that. No."

"But I really—"

He stuck his palm up, cutting her off. "It's not up

for negotiation. Benjamin?"

Benjamin stepped into the hall from the kitchen. Jeez, these two were never more than a few feet from each other. "Need something?"

"Can you get some beignets for Stacia?"

"Of course." Benjamin disappeared, and Stacia had no doubt he'd magically produce exactly what Walker requested.

"That's not what I meant. I want to go get them. Besides, everyone knows beignets are best out of the fryer."

"I'm going down for a workout. Enjoy your beignets." Walker disappeared, leaving her alone in the kitchen.

She opened her mouth to protest but knew it wouldn't do her any good. She slumped into the stool at the kitchen counter and listened to his footsteps descend the staircase. Stacia hated the fact she needed permission to do something as simple as taking a stroll. There was no reason she couldn't go by herself. She wasn't a child. In the span of a handful of days, she'd gone from being an independent woman to having to ask to get a cup of coffee. Even worse, only days ago she'd shared the most intimate experience she'd ever had with a man who could barely look at her now. She refused to let him see how much that fact was breaking her heart.

She spotted Walker's Saints baseball cap hanging from the door and a pair of sunglasses on the counter. "Fuck this." She shoved the cap on her head, tucking her hair inside, grabbed a pair of glasses and slipped out the side door. After she punched in the code she'd memorized from watching Walker disarm the alarm, the patio gate opened. Stacia pulled it closed behind her and stepped onto the sidewalk suddenly feeling lighter than she had since she arrived in New Orleans.

She took a deep breath, inhaling the sweet aroma of flowers and sunlight as she headed toward St. Charles Avenue. Standing at the trolley stop with the other morning commuters and tourists, she felt like she'd rejoined life, making her feel almost normal again. But as the minutes ticked by her heart raced as she wondered if she'd spot Walker or Benjamin, or perhaps both, rushing across the street to apprehend her and drag her back to the house. Relief filled her body when the trolley squealed to a halt and she stepped aboard. Stacia pulled her hat off for a moment to allow the breeze to blow through her hair. The trolley stopped at almost each block, as people came and left. Confident she'd put enough distance between herself and the house on Prytania Road, she jumped off at a stop near a bakery. Stacia decided to forego her initial choice of taking a seat at a table on the sidewalk. On the outside chance Walker had followed her, she'd at least give him a challenge of finding her. Stacia ordered a beignet and coffee at the counter and claimed a small table in the corner where she could keep her eye on the door. As she sank her teeth into the flaky pastry, the flavors mingled with her taste buds. She licked the powdered sugar from her lips and sipped her coffee. A tinge of guilt traveled through her gut when her eyes tipped to the empty chair. By then, Walker would've discovered she left the house alone and she was sure he was pissed. Not only had she gone against his request, she, in his opinion, had put herself in danger. Part of the reason she'd gone against his wishes was the fact that he'd been so cold to her since their scene in the Tower Room. He'd treated her like a stranger ever since learning her father was one of his agents. It's like he erased their night together from mind, and it hurt her more than she was willing to admit.

Screw Walker. She could take care of herself just

fine. She didn't need him. Stacia scanned the bakery. There was certainly not one suspicious looking person in the place. Just families wearing NOLA shirts, a few people in business attire grabbing a coffee to go, and a couple of retiree aged folks enjoying a leisurely breakfast, and not one of them resembled a mobster. She popped the last of the beignet into her mouth and carried her cup outside. She resisted the urge to meander through the neighboring shops and instead headed back to the trolley stop. She'd proved her point by going out for breakfast without incident. Walker couldn't argue with the facts, although she knew he would. But that would be a good thing. Maybe he'd be so relieved when she returned that he'd actually talk to her again.

Standing at the corner, a bookshop across the street caught her eye and beckoned her inside. A few more minutes wouldn't hurt. She crossed the street and grasped the knob of a weathered door. A bell jingled as she stepped inside. She scanned the tiny shop crammed with floor to ceiling shelves.

"Good morning," a voice called.

Stacia craned her head around a shelf and spotted the source of the voice. "Oh, hello." She smiled at an old man behind the counter at the back of the shop. The large antique cash register almost hid his body.

"Looking for something in particular?" he asked.

"Just browsing for now." She ran her fingers across the spines of new books mixed with old. Contemporaries and cozy mysteries sat side by side with biographies and cookbooks. "Um, do you have anything about the history of New Orleans architecture? My boyfriend bought a fixer-upper in the Garden District." She smiled at the comparison of the Prytania house to a "fixer-upper" as well as Walker as her "boyfriend". Both couldn't be further from the truth.

He pointed a crooked finger toward a series of shelves. "I think there's one or two on that shelf behind you."

Stacia turned and scanned the shelf. A shiver ran through her when her gaze passed *Mafia Killers* in search of a book on architecture. "I don't see it."

"Maybe one over. Here, I'll show you…" He started a slow hobble toward the shelf when the brass bell above the door tinkled. The man's gaze shifted to the door. "Welcome, sir. Looking for something in particular?"

"In fact, I am," he said.

Stacia froze. Her view was blocked, but she knew it was Jake who'd entered the store. She'd never forget his voice.

"I need to help this young lady first," the old man said, still making his way to the shelf.

"I'm sure I can find it myself," Jake said from the door.

Stacia scanned the store for another way out. She grabbed the old man's wrist. "Is there a backdoor?"

"Eh? Sorry, I didn't hear you." He cupped his hand to his ear.

"A backdoor."

A dark form appeared behind the old man. "The only way out is through me and this."

Stacia's gaze tipped to the pistol in his hand. The old man continued squinting at the spines of books on the shelf.

"Surprised to see me?" Jake laughed. "Of course you are. You and your boyfriend think you're so smart, but we knew where you were the whole time and it was just a matter of time before you did something like this. I knew you would if we held out long enough. You don't like doing what you're told. He doesn't even know you're gone, does he?" He spoke in a hushed voice too low for the seemingly hard of hearing bookstore owner to hear.

She had to think fast. "Of course he does. He's on his way here now."

"You're lying, but that doesn't matter. You'll be long gone by the time he gets here."

The old man turned around, and Jake hid the gun inside his jacket. "I'll be with you in a moment, sir."

Jake strode past the man and swung his arm around Stacia's shoulders. "Thanks, but I found what I was looking for," Jake said before tilting his face toward Stacia's ear. "We're going to walk out of the shop quietly together. If you try anything stupid I'll shoot the old man. Got it?"

She nodded. "One sec." She pulled a book from the shelf. "Please hold this for me." Stacia handed the old man the book and allowed Jake to lead her to the door.

"Wait, this isn't..." the man called as the bell rang a final time before she was dragged to the waiting car outside.

Chapter Sixteen

His heart dropped as Walker stepped out of another bakery. It must've been the tenth one he'd tried. He and Benjamin had both searched for Stacia on foot and hit every beignet place within a five-mile radius. One clerk thought she was in the shop earlier but he couldn't be sure. Every minute that went by, every dead end, felt like she was slipping further away. *Damn it.* Why didn't she listen to him and stay put? He tightened his fists. Worse was how he didn't anticipate her leaving the house. He should never have let her out of his sight.

Benjamin held his phone to his ear and held up his index finger. "Right. Did he say anything else? What's the address? Thanks." He dropped the phone on the table. "Our source at the NOPD said a shop owner stopped a uniform on the sidewalk a few minutes ago and told him about a woman who had come into the shop. A big guy came in a few minutes later and practically dragged her out and into a waiting car. She fit Stacia's description and had on a Saints cap. The shop is down a couple blocks."

Walker nodded. "Let's go."

Walker and Benjamin entered the crammed shop.

"What do you two want because you don't look like you're interested in a book." An old man shuffled from behind the counter. Deep lines decorated his face. "If you're looking for trouble, I'll call the cops."

Walker held up his hands. "No trouble, sir. But my friend is in some. I think she was here not too long ago. Pretty woman wearing a Saints cap?"

He nodded, his concerned gaze bouncing from Walker to Benjamin. "I was helping her look for a book on New Orleans architecture. She said she wanted to give it to her boyfriend because he was renovating a historic house in the Garden District." He tipped his chin to Walker. "You him? Her boyfriend?"

He'd never thought of himself as boyfriend material, but the label suddenly felt right when it came to Stacia. "Yeah, that's me."

"Lucky guy. What type of trouble is she in?"

"I'm not sure. What can you tell me about her visit?"

The man twisted his mouth in thought. "Not much. She was only here for a few minutes. She looked around, asked me about the book, and then some big guy in black came in and said he found what he was looking for. He grabbed her and left."

"Did she leave willingly?"

"That's the thing. I'm not sure. I mean she didn't put up a fight, but there was terror in her eyes. She looked scared. She tried to ask me something, but I couldn't hear her. My hearing isn't what it used to be."

Walker's nails cut into his palm as he tightened his fist again. He wanted to punch someone. He should've been there to protect her. He ran his palm down his face. "Anything else you can think of?"

The old man was silent for a long moment. "Yeah, there's something else. She asked me to hold a book for her, but it wasn't the type of book she was looking for."

"May we see it?" Benjamin asked.

"It's right here, under the counter." He lifted a hardcover book from under the counter. A piece of scratch paper was secured to the cover with a rubber band. Walker read the unsteady handwriting: **Girl With Saints Cap**

The man shrugged. "I never got her name."

Walker pulled aside the paper and read the title *Mafia Killers*.

"I thought it was a strange book for someone like her to want."

Walker turned the cover toward Benjamin. She'd left them a sign.

"Carlo has her," Benjamin said. "Thank you. This was very helpful," Benjamin said to the old man as Walker rushed to the door.

Chapter Seventeen

"Wake up, sweetheart."

Stacia groaned when something hard slammed into her ribs. A shoe? She rolled onto her side and tried to get up but her hands were stretched over her head and tied to something. The scent of a musty rug invaded her nostrils as she tried to open her eyes. Everything hurt, even her eyelids.

"Where am I?" she croaked out.

A chuckle sounded above her. "Vegas, baby."

Stacia froze, and her mind raced. How he hell did she get to Vegas? "What?" She blinked, and she made out two thick legs standing in front of her face.

"You don't remember anything, do ya? That's some good shit you're on. Addictive as fuck, too. All Carlo's girls are on it."

That explained why her body felt like it was run over by a train. "What is it?" Her words were like chewing gum in her mouth, all jumbled up and sticky. She needed to clear the fog from her head. She needed air.

A rattle sounded above her. "Flow-ni-traz … I don't know. Whatever the fuck it is, I'm supposed to give you another one."

Flunitrazepam. She'd edited a story about it. Street name "Roofies". The date rape drug of choice. A meaty hand stinking like stale cigars grabbed her jaw and tried to pry her mouth open. She turned her head to the side. "Please. Just let me up or I'm going to be sick."

"Jee-suz. Bad enough I gotta babysit you. I ain't cleaning your puke, too."

The guy huffed to her head and unknotted the rope that held her arms down but kept her wrists bound together. Her hands felt as though they were holding lead weights as she dragged them to her chest and tried to sit. The lead moved to her head, which she couldn't lift from the floor.

"Here." The meaty hand was back and tugged her arm until she was in a sitting position.

It took all of her concentration to keep her head steady and focus her gaze on the face of the burly man at her side. "Who are you?"

"Name's Bruno. You must be pretty important to be in Carlo's office. The other new girls are brought downstairs." His eyes trailed her body. "But a girl you're not. You a little old for Carlo."

She scanned her surroundings. Her vision was still fuzzy, but she could make out a wood desk and a set of leather chairs behind Bruno. Nausea overwhelmed her, and the room started to spin.

"Whoa. I said no puking. Here." He grabbed her ankles and swiveled her so she faced him. "Lean back." Her back rested against a sofa. "Better?"

She nodded. "Can I have some water?"

"Have some right here. You gotta take one of these, too. Carlo's orders."

He shook a pill from the container and twisted the cap off a water bottle. "Open up."

Stacia had no choice but to let him drop the pill into her mouth. With her tongue, she lodged the pill between her back molars and cheek before he tipped the bottle to her lips.

"You swallowed it, right? Open up."

She opened her mouth and managed to also lift her tongue without revealing the hidden pill. Through her research, she remembered the reason roofies were the date rape drug of choice. They were soluble, which meant she had a few seconds to spit the pill out before it dissolved in her mouth. When he turned his back to place the bottle on the desk she turned her head to cough and the pill dropped to the carpet. She managed to nudge it under the sofa with her bound hands. Bruno turned his interest back to her and stared at her hands. "What are you doing?"

"Stretching. I can't feel my hands." She purposely slurred her words.

She couldn't be sure the pill was out of sight, and dread fell over her when he squinted at the floor next to where she was seated. A muffled sound distracted Bruno, and he fished inside his jacket and pulled out a phone. "Yeah… Okay… Got it." He shoved the device back in his pocket and lumbered toward Stacia. "Boss wants to talk to you." He pulled her to her feet and guided her to the desk. "Sit." He nudged her into the chair as she heard the door open.

The door squealed behind her shoulder. "You can go now, Bruno." A soft but gruff voice sounded.

"Yes, sir." The door clicked closed as a slight man with a shock of white hair moved into her view. He looked more like someone's frail grandfather than the kingpin of the world's most powerful crime organization.

"A pleasure to finally meet you, Ms. Howell. I'm sure you know who I am." Stacia noticed a residual old Italian accent she was sure he tried to erase over the years but couldn't rid himself of it completely. He walked around the desk, and the air wheezed from his lungs as he sat in a worn leather chair.

"What do you want from me?" she asked, drawing her words out, giving him no reason to doubt whether the drug was in her system.

Carlo leaned his elbows on the desk's surface and laced his fingers together. "It's not what I want from you. It's what I want from Mark Platinum."

"Never met him."

"On the contrary, my dear. I have pictures of you getting up close and personal with him on his motorcycle."

Even with the ball of cotton still spinning in her head from the lingering drug, she was sure she heard him right. Pictures of her with Mark Platinum?

A smug smile crossed his wrinkled lips as he rose. "Mark *Walker* Platinum," he said slowly. "He didn't tell you who he was, did he?"

Her head swirled. Walker was Mark Platinum? Why didn't he tell her? What else was he hiding?

"Don't be too disappointed. Men like Mark have a goal. Power. Nothing else matters. Everything and everyone else is dispensable. It's why I haven't been able to destroy him." He paused and wheezed a shallow breath. "Yet. But I finally have something he wants." He paused, and he pointed a gnarled finger in her direction. "You. You belong to one of his agents and he failed to keep you safe so he'll come to collect you. It's a matter of honor."

Collect her, like a possession. Was that how her father thought of her, too? The tattoo on her father's chest that matched Walker's flashed in her head. It was strange to think of her father's connection with Walker. There was much about him, about both of them, she didn't know.

Carlo studied her face for more than a few seconds. "But now that you're here I may as well put you to work. All of my girls need to earn their keep."

Her heart revved into overdrive, but she refused to show how much he rattled her nerves so simply stared into his icy eyes. "And how might I do that?"

Carlo picked up his phone. His gold ring encrusted with diamonds sparkled as he flashed a yellowed tooth smile in Stacia's direction. "Please send

Lady Elinor to my office. We have a guest who needs to borrow something from our wardrobe."

They sat in silence, giving Stacia a moment to come up with a plan. Something. Anything to get her the hell away. Stacia willed herself not to jump when the door swung open and heavy footsteps lumbered into the room.

"You never told me you were expecting a guest." A deep but feminine voice rang from behind. Stacia turned to find one of the tallest women she'd ever seen standing in the doorway with her arms crossed. "I'm already up to my tits with these newbies. Now there's another one?" Her blood-red nails waved in Stacia's direction like she was some orphaned kitten.

Carlo fished around a desk drawer before lumbering upright and walking around his desk. A blade flashed from his hand which he used to cut the bounds from Stacia's wrists. "Show her to the dressing room and give her something to wear. She's performing for my personal guests tonight."

Elinor huffed out an audible breath. "Come with me."

Stacia stood and opened her mouth to protest but decided she'd have a greater chance escaping Elinor's clutches than Carlo's locked and guarded office. Stacia tried to memorize the club's floor plan as Elinor shuffled her down the stairs, through the marbled hallway of the main floor and down another staircase.

A shiver crawled up her spine. Going upstairs was more comforting to Stacia than being below the ground floor. Bad things happened in basements. People were murdered in basements. Didn't Hannibal Lecter keep his victims there? Stacia hesitated at the top of the stairs. Elinor stopped and swung her head to the side, her thick red hair following over her shoulder. "Waiting for something?"

During the past few days, Stacia had barely had the opportunity to use the bathroom without Walker or Benjamin trailing close behind. What she wouldn't give to have them show up at that second. She sucked back a sob and lowered her foot to the first stair.

Chapter Eighteen

Elinor pulled a set of keys from a band around her wrist and unlocked a door at the bottom of the stairs. "There's a rack of costumes in here. Hurry up and pick something," she ordered, holding the door ajar.

Stacia stepped into what looked like the locker room at her gym except this one had a clothing rack of slinky clothes and a counter filled with hairbrushes and various cosmetics.

A muffled ringtone echoed through the room. Elinor pulled her phone from her pocket, and poked the screen. "Yes? ... Jeez-us. Can't you handle it?" Elinor spat. "Okay. Be right there." She shook her head, shoved the phone back in her pocket, and glared at Stacia. "Find something to wear and pretty yourself up. You need some eye makeup." She narrowed her eyes and her nose wrinkled. "A lot of eye makeup. I will be right back." The door slammed shut followed by a click of a lock.

It was the first time she'd been left by herself since she entered the club, and she had to find a way out before Medusa returned. She scanned the room, which contained a row of toilet stalls and a couple showers to one side and a dressing area with cabinets on the other. The locked door was the only way in and out. She gripped the counter with both hands, deciding her next move when she heard what sounded like a sniffle across the room. She followed the sound and a rustle of fabric filled her ears.

"Hello? Is someone in here?" Peering into each stall she continued down the row. She pushed open the third stall, and a whimper filled her ears. "Who's there?" She reached the last door and stopped short at the sight before her.

A girl sat on the tank with her bare feet on the

toilet seat. She hugged her arms to her chest, her body trembling like hunted prey. The girl lifted her tearstained face to Stacia. Stacia sucked in a breath. She couldn't be a day older than sixteen.

"Oh my God," Stacia said and stepped inside the stall. "Are you okay? Did they hurt you?" She reached out to touch the girl's hand, but she pulled it away. "I'm not going to hurt you." Stacia smoothed the girl's hair from her face, and her eyes trained on a dark bruise under her eye. "Holy shit." Her head raced, shuffling through ideas on how to get this girl out of the club. "What's your name, honey?" Stacia asked.

The girl shook her head.

"Your name?" she repeated. Still nothing. She didn't understand. Stacia remembered Jake talking about going to Mexico. God, it all made sense. The Cardinellis were kidnapping girls from Mexico and smuggling them into the States to work at places like The Silver Club. She tried to recall her high school Spanish. "Um, *tu nombre?*"

The girl's eyes met hers. "L-Leena."

Stacia nodded. "*Bueno.*" She put her hand on her chest. "I'm Stacia. I'm going to get you out of here." She stroked her hair. "How old are you, sweetheart? *Cuantos anos?*"

"*Catorce.*"

"*Catorce.*" Stacia touched her fingers as she counted in her head. *Diez, once, doce, trece, catorce.* Her heart pounded. "You're only fourteen. Oh, my God. Oh, my God. Okay … okay." She pinched the bridge of her nose with her thumb and index finger, hoping a plan would plant itself into her head. The clink of metal echoed through the room, and Stacia put her index finger to her lips. Heavy footsteps sounded and stopped. Stacia took a deep breath and plastered her best smile on her face before stepping out of the stall.

"You're not dressed yet?" Elinor asked.

Stacia wobbled toward the woman to move her focus away from the stall. "I can't do it. Not feeling well."

Elinor raised her eyebrows. "Carlo won't be happy about that. A few of his special clients like their girls on the older side. You'll do with some makeup."

"Maybe after some rest. Can I lay down somewhere?" Stacia's gaze moved to the opened door, weighing the chances of knocking Elinor on her ass and finding her way out of the club. *Slim to none.*

"This isn't a day spa, girl. Squeeze your ass into one of those dresses and let's go." Elinor bellowed. A shuffle sounded in the direction of the stalls, and she caught Elinor's eyes tracking toward the noise.

Stacia threw her arms in the air. "Okay. Fine. You win. Show me what to wear." She led Elinor to the rack of clothes. Anything to get the woman away from little Leena and buy Stacia some time to figure out how to the hell out of there.

Elinor's meaty fingers pawed through the rack of cheap spandex and rhinestone dresses. She held it to Stacia's chest. "This one. It should be big enough for you." Stacia surveyed the low-cut mermaid blood red gown. She'd have a hell of a time running for her life in that thing.

"Red's not my color."

Elinor huffed. "I don't care what you wear. Get yourself together and knock on the door when you're ready. You have three minutes," Elinor said with a sneer before she strode from the room and slammed the door.

Stacia raced to the stall hiding Leena. "Stay here and stay quiet. I'll get you out of here." She touched her index finger to her lips. A small nod confirmed she at least understood the quiet part. Stacia ran back, pulled a short blue number from a hanger, shed her clothes, and stepped into the dress. Surveying herself in the mirror, she swiped a coat of red gloss on her lips and sparkly shadow on her eyelids.

"Please, Walker. Hurry," she muttered as she stepped into the hallway wondering how many other girls were kept inside the club and what type of hell they were going through. Her stomach lurched at the possibilities crawling into her head.

Chapter Nineteen

Following Elinor, Stacia scanned the hallway as they passed a series of closed doors. Were there more girls locked behind them? Her gaze trailed to the ceiling and steadied on a dark glass dome. Cameras. She figured the entire club was filled with them. How the hell was she going to get back downstairs to Leena and how many more girls like her were locked away?

"Stop dragging your feet, girl," Elinor grumbled.

Stacia considered ambushing the woman from behind but quickly dispelled the thought. It didn't take a sports bookie to know the odds weren't in her favor. Elinor's height and brawn would take Stacia down in a quick second. Plus, she still had the residual effects of roofies swimming in her head. She was ushered to a door on the main floor and pushed inside. A rumbling of voices quieted as she moved farther into the room the stench of cigarettes and cigars overtook her sense leaving her even more queasy.

"May I introduce Miss Stacia," Elinor said before closing the door, leaving all eyes on Stacia.

"We've been waiting for you." Carlo's voice sounded from the corner, but Stacia couldn't see him through the dim light and smoke.

She straightened her spine and took a calming breath, trying to slow her pounding heart. "I'm not feeling well. I'd like to lay down."

"Just some nerves. Everyone has them the first time," he said.

She swallowed the bile rising in her throat as she scanned the room in search of another way out.

Carlo chuckled. "I promised these men a show. You don't want to disappoint them, do you? Maybe what you need is a drink."

She nodded as she continued to step around the tables of seated men who seemed to be undressing her with their eyes. "Yes. Water, please." There had to be a way out.

Finally, Carlo stood from his seat at the front table with a glass in his hand. He moved to her side and curled his palm around her elbow. "Drink this."

Ice cubes clinked against the glass as she took the drink from his hand and brought it to her lips. She sealed her lip to the glass and pretended to take a sip. She licked her lips detecting a residual metallic taste. "What is this?"

"Something to calm your nerves, Stacia. Now how about you honor us with a dance. The stage is ready for you." He nodded to a gleaming silver pole stuck in the middle of a narrow platform at the front of the room. "Start the music," he called, and a fast, electric beat poured into the room. She kicked off her shoes and stepped onto the platform as a bright spotlight swung in her direction. Her head started to spin, and sweat formed on her upper lip and forehead. She hooked her arm around the pole and spun around once. Her head continued to spin even when she stopped and scanned the crowd in search of someone, anyone who could help her. She spotted Elinor striding toward Carlo. She appeared to be shouting something with her hand curled over his ear before Elinor threw a sneer in Stacia's direction.

"Everyone out!" Carlo's voice roared above the noise.

The music stopped, and a few boos filled the silence as most of the men filed out the doors. Stacia held the pole to keep her from falling. It was as if she were riding an out of control merry-go-round. She sank to the ground and leaned her face on the metal pole, cooling her heated cheek. Willing her eyes to open, her gaze landed on Carlo as he approached her with two men at either side. "Elinor tells me you met another one of our guests downstairs."

An icy shiver ran up her spine. "She's just a child."

"Miss Leena was supposed to entertain one of my special members tonight. Because of you she's a blubbering mess and won't be able to do her job, so we'll need someone to take her place."

A surge of energy filled Stacia. She pushed to her feet using the pole to steady her body. "Fuck you," she spat and trained her eyes on the door. Either she'd get out or she'd die trying. Being raped wasn't an option.

"I'm not the lucky man tonight, but you'll meet him soon. First you need to finish the rest of your drink."

Hands grabbed her from behind, and Elinor wrapped her arm around Stacia's neck while tipping her head back. She clamped her mouth shut as the woman's nails clawed her lips open. Stacia sputtered and tried not to swallow, but what ended up down her throat hit her brain like a Mack truck almost immediately. Blurry colors and shapes filled her head and voices came and went. She tried to fight, to lift her fist, but her body wouldn't cooperate.

"Walker," she whispered before darkness took over.

Chapter Twenty

"What's our ETA?" Walker barked.

"The same as when you asked five minutes ago. Thirty minutes to touchdown," Benjamin answered from his seat.

Within an hour of leaving the bookstore, a Platinum informant reported a private plane leaving in a hurry destined for Las Vegas. It was Carlo's style to stick it to Walker by taking Stacia hostage in the exact place he acquired from Platinum. Stacia could only be in one place: The Silver Club.

"Get Potter on the phone. He should be there by now." Nash Potter, ex-Navy Seal with a chip on his shoulder as big as a hockey puck, was one of Platinum's best agents. Walker had planned for Potter's next assignment to be guarding Stacia when she resumed her life in LA, but that plan flew out the window when Stacia walked out the door.

Benjamin pointed to his tablet. "I have his location on GPS. He'll make it to Vegas about the same time we will. He can't go in alone anyway."

Walker paced the cabin. A ball of rage tightened in his belly. He'd never felt so helpless. He always had a fix for any problem, which could usually be solved by throwing money at the source. In this case, the Cardinellis didn't need his money. They had enough of their own. They had something of Walker's. Not just something. Some*one*. And within the span of a few days she'd nestled under his skin and suddenly there was no way he would be able to live without her. *Fuck me*. The knot in his gut felt like it exploded into a million shards of glass when visions of what they could be doing to her flashed in his mind. He knew what they were capable of. He'd spent most of his career trying to take them down.

They preyed on the weak and susceptible. However, Stacia was neither, and he could only hope that would work in her favor … and his.

"She's strong, Walker. She has balls of steel stronger than any man I know. Including you."

Walker turned toward Benjamin to throw a retort his way, but truth was, Benjamin was right. It was also what worried him the most. Stacia's spunk was no match for the Cardinelli organization.

"Prepare for landing, Mr. Platinum," the pilot's voice rang through the speaker.

He sank into his seat and mentally ran through the plan. "This isn't going to be easy. You ready to do this, Benjamin?" he asked, even though he already knew the answer.

"For a long time, there was only one person I'd take a bullet for. Now there are two," Benjamin said evenly as they made their descent into the desert.

Walker spotted the waiting car on the tarmac as the plane landed. Every second counted from this moment forward. "Where's Potter?"

"He's a few minutes away. He'll meet us in a parking lot across from the club. But someone else answered your call for backup."

Walker flicked his gaze around the chair. There were only a handful of Platinum agents, but most were on assignment in the Caribbean and the East Coast. Walker sent details of the situation to all but one agent. He knew chances were less than zero any of them would be able to get to Vegas in time to help the rescue effort, but he needed to keep them on notice, especially if something went wrong. "Who?"

Benjamin met his stare. "Nighthawk."

He narrowed his eyes. "I told you I kept him out of it."

"She's his daughter, Walker. He has the right to know."

"Cardinelli knows the connection. It's why he targeted Stacia. He's drawing us in to destroy us. To destroy Platinum. I left Nighthawk out to keep him protected."

"You sure about that? It's not because you feel responsible for the kidnapping? For not keeping your promise to him to keep her safe?" Benjamin asked.

The question hung in the air as the plane touched down.

Walker turned toward the window catching his reflection. His jaw tightened as Benjamin's words sank in. "You think this is my fault?"

Benjamin cleared his throat. "No. But *you* do."

Walker unbuckled his seatbelt. "She was my responsibility. I promised her father I'd protect her," he said quietly.

"I think there's more to it. You have feelings for her, and that scares the crap out of you."

"What are you, my therapist now, Benjamin?"

"Spend enough time with someone and you get to know them better than they know themselves."

Benjamin was right again. But his feelings for Stacia were the reason her life sat in Carlo's hands, and he felt so fucking helpless.

"There he is." Benjamin pointed to a tall figure standing next to their car.

Walker studied the man as Benjamin opened the jet's door and the portable stairs were secured in place. He'd only seen him from the shoulders up on a monitor. He judged his age at about seventy with a full head of grey hair and deep lines decorating his face. However, his broad shoulders and quick pace defied his apparent age. Nighthawk met Walker and Benjamin at the bottom of the stairs. "Let's forgo the pleasantries in lieu of a briefing."

"First, I must apologize. Stacia was in my care, and I let her out of my sight."

"I know my daughter better than anyone. Keeping her put is like holding sand in your palm. Stacia does what she wants. I was never able to control her actions and nor will you. Better learn that now."

"I still feel responsible."

"And so do I. Which is why I'm here. Let's go get her. I'll tell you what I learned about Carlo's operations in the car," Nighthawk said.

Walker followed Nighthawk into the backseat as Benjamin climbed into the front passenger side. "About a week ago, twelve girls were kidnapped from their school in Nogales. The Mexican authorities have been tightlipped about it. No media footage and no investigation was opened."

"The local cops are being paid off," Walker said.

"Exactly and it wasn't the first time. The situation has Carlo Cardinelli stench all over it."

"You think he has the girls at The Silver Club."

"I don't think it. I know it. Someone made an anonymous call to the Vegas PD. The guy had passed out in his car the night before and woke to see a bunch of girls being brought into the club with their hands tied."

"Shit." Walker raked his fingers over his face. On top of saving Stacia, which would be as easy as stealing the queen's jewels from Buckingham Palace, they'd need to also extract twelve underage girls from the building. *Sure. It would be a cakewalk.* "Benjamin, pull up the club's floorplan on your tablet."

Benjamin handed Walker the screen, and Walker took Nighthawk through his plan.

"You're going through the front door?"

Nighthawk asked.

Walker nodded. "My bet is most of the members and Cardinelli soldiers are in the front two rooms. I'll create a scene from the entrance while Benjamin and Potter go through the side door. It's only a few feet away to the basement access. There's a locker room and a bunch of small rooms down there." Walker decided it was the best place to start. With any luck, they'd yank Stacia and the girls out before the Cardinellis knew what hit them. But Walker knew it wouldn't be that simple. The chances they'd all be in the same place were slim to none. The club was huge, with three floors, offices and private suites. Stacia could be anywhere inside. The air squeezed from his lungs when he let his mind drift to what they could be doing to her at that moment.

"What happens if the basement is empty?" Nighthawk asked.

"Benjamin and Potter cover me and we move upstairs."

The older man's sharp gaze moved from Walker to Benjamin. "That's it? Your plan is a death sentence."

"You have a better one?"

"We need backup."

Walker shook his head. "The local and state police are overrun with Cardinelli spies. I don't want the Feds involved yet. There's too much risk of a leak. We can't chance getting them involved until we get Stacia and the girls out."

"Fine, but what's my role in this?" Nighthawk asked.

"Outside waiting. We'll need help when we bring the girls out. You can contact the police after they're recused."

"Don't be a fool, Walker. You need me inside. Every second you remain inside the club your chances of getting out reduce exponentially."

"With all due respect, sir. You aren't in your twenties anymore."

"I'm not a weak link, Walker," he said quietly. "She's my daughter. I want in."

Walker stared into the man's eyes and realized they had something else in common other than Platinum. They both loved the woman they were trying to save.

Walker clapped him on the shoulder. "I can use another man on the inside. We're in this together."

Chapter Twenty-One

Walker's heart drummed in his chest as his boots crunched the graveled parking lot. He palmed the pistol in the concealed holster at his side. Death wasn't something he was afraid of. He'd come within a whisper more than a few times. It was the other lives that hung over his head that drove him to not accept anything but success in this mission. Benjamin, Potter, and Nighthawk, willingly putting their lives on the lines to save Stacia. He couldn't let them down. He wouldn't let *her* down. Walker scanned the exterior of the club as he approached and his thoughts turned to Stacia and the young girls inside. If ever there was a time he wished for x-ray vision this was it. His gut told him they'd find the girls in the basement, but he knew Carlo would keep Stacia close. Carlo hated to be made to look like a fool, especially a second time. Extracting Stacia from Cardinelli claws without bloodshed was probably not an option. He only hoped the blood was Cardinelli's.

"Can I help you, sir?" the man at the door asked as he approached.

"You can tell Carlo I came to take back what's mine." In one fluid stroke, he twisted the man's arm behind his back and rested his gun against the man's temple. "On second thought, I'll tell him myself." Walker pushed the man through the door into a dimly lit room. "Listen up! I want Carlo Cardinelli now or this guy's brain will be splattered across the bar," Walker called. A few men ran into the darkness at the back of the room. Walker knew it exited to a hallway. The rest of the members backed against the walls or ducked under tables. The guy tried to break free, and Walker held him tighter. "Don't test me. I'm in the mood to kill someone today," he grumbled. "Where do they keep the girls?"

"What girls?"

"We can do this the easy way or I can put a bullet through your skull. You know what girls." He couldn't see shit as he squinted through the haze of smoke floating in the stale air. "Where's Carlo?" he called out. "My finger's getting itchy."

"I wondered when you'd show up, Platinum," Carlo said as he appeared from the shadows. "I see your girlfriend slipped your leash, too. She's more trouble than she's worth. How about I do us both a favor and we'll take care of her after she entertains my members?"

Rage coursed through Walker's veins. He knew Carlo was trying to provoke him. He swallowed his fury. "Let her go and I'll let your man live," he said evenly.

"Stacia's a little incapacitated right now," Carlo said with a crooked smile.

Walker's eyes burned as the fire fought its way back. "What the fuck did you do to her?"

Carlo chuckled. "Let's just say she couldn't keep her eyes open after the night she's had servicing our members."

Walker grip tightened, and he twisted the guard's arm until he cried out. "If you touched her, if anyone here touched her, I will spend the rest of my life making you pay. Where is she?"

"You have a soft spot for her, Platinum. In your business that's a fatal mistake. She'll be your downfall." Carlo pointed a crooked finger at Walker. "Why do you think I targeted her? Love makes you blind to what's in front of your face."

Another man Walker recognized as Jake grabbed Carlo's shoulder. "We have to get you out of here, Carlo."

"No one leaves until I find Stacia or you'll have one less man." Walker twisted his captive's arm.

"You overestimate me. Men like this one pledge their loyalty to me but they're dispensable. There are fifty other men out there willing to take his place," Carlo said, flashing a row of yellowing teeth.

Walker narrowed his eyes deciding whether to call the crime boss's bluff. A drop of sweat trickled down the man's neck. In one fluid move, Walker spun him around and grabbed the man's gun from the holster under his jacket before pushing him to the floor. With a gun in each hand, he pointed them at Jake and Carlo. "You're going to turn around and lead me to Stacia. Now."

His eyes tipped to Jake's hand reaching to his hip, Walker's finger hugged the trigger as he caught the flash of metal in Jake's hand. He narrowed his eyes on his target and fired as he was slammed in the back of his knees, leveling him to the ground. The gunshot echoed, and a stampede of footsteps pounded toward the exit. Walker watched as Jake shielded Carlo and hurried him from the room. Rolling to his side, Walker's eyes landed on his attacker. "I fucking saved you from your employer."

"And I returned the favor. Jake wasn't the only one with a gun. There was a target on your head from across the room," the man said as he stood and offered a hand to Walker.

Walker accepted it and moved to his feet. "What's your name?"

"Bruno. Come on, we only have a few minutes while they hustle Carlo outta here. I think they have your girl upstairs."

Walker scanned the empty room, but his gaze caught movement through the doorway leading to the hallway.

"Walker, we got most of the girls out but no sign of Stacia downstairs or on this floor!" Walker followed the direction of Benjamin's voice. When he found him in the hallway, Walker waved him off as he pointed his gun at Bruno. "It's okay. He's helping us. Says she's upstairs. What do you mean, most of them?"

"Potter and Nighthawk are still breaking down doors down there," Benjamin said.

"Bruno, go to the basement and help my guys get the rest of the girls out. We'll get Stacia." As much as he could use Bruno's knowledge of the club's floorplan, Walker wanted Benjamin by his side.

"Turn left at the top of the stairs and try the first door on the left. That's Carlo's office." Bruno nodded and disappeared down the stairwell as Walker's gaze traveled up the other. "We don't have much time. More of Carlo's men will be back."

Benjamin waved his gun toward the second floor. "Let's go get her."

Walker headed up first and crouched as he got to the top of the stairs. He scanned both directions before signaling to Benjamin to cover one side of the door and he took the other. He put his ear to the wall straining to hear anything. The silence sliced through him. If she was inside, he hoped to hear crying, or yelling, or sounds of her trying to escape. Not silence. It meant something was wrong. He turned ready to crash it open with his foot when Benjamin raised his hand and shook his head. He pointed to a strip of metal along the seam of the door and then to the small panel on the wall. In Walker's haste to get Stacia the hell out of there, he'd neglected common sense. The crime boss's door was reinforced and digitally secure. There was no way he was breaking in the old-fashioned way. Benjamin pulled his phone from his pocket and tapped the screen a few times before holding the device to the panel.

"How long's this going to take?" Walker said in a

frustrated whisper.

Benjamin's eyes steadied on his phone screen. "Ready to go in three … two … one." A soft click sounded and the door opened a crack. Walker swung his arm inside with gun in hand and stepped inside. He scanned the room and fire scorched his eyes when his stare met the surprised gaze of a half-naked man leaning over a body on a sofa. *Let it not be her.* But his worst nightmare slammed into his head when Walker's gaze landed on the pair of red soled heels on the victim's feet. His heart dropped. The last time he'd seen those shoes they were on Stacia the last night they were together. "Get the fuck away from her!" Walker roared as he stormed to the sofa and pulled the man up by his hair.

Walker's hand shook in rage as he jabbed the muzzle of his pistol against the man's fleshy cheek.

The man's hands flew in the air. "I'm sorry! Please don't shoot me. Please."

Walker tightened his grip on the man's hair, eliciting a sob from the sweaty ball of scum. His focus moved to Stacia and his brain shattered. A strip of duct tape covered her mouth. "Jesus." He threw the man to the ground and knelt at Stacia's side. Dark circles were etched under her closed eyes. Walker ripped the tape from her mouth and felt for a pulse as his eyes flicked to Benjamin, whose worried expression mirrored his own. He bent down and angled his cheek to her face as a faint but strong beat hit his fingers and shallow breaths blanketed his face. "She's breathing." He pointed his gun at the man. "You fucking animal. What did you do to her?"

"Nothing. She was like this when I came in. Carlo said she was my date tonight but nothing happened. I swear."

"You piece of shit." His voice shook as he spoke.

"Did you…" He couldn't spit the words out.

"No. No. I swear. She's passed out." His meaty hand waved weakly over Stacia's body.

"And I'm about to send you to hell," Walker said, hooking his finger over the trigger.

"Don't do it, Walker. You don't need his blood on your hands," Benjamin said. "Your war is with Carlo."

Walker lowered his gun and swallowed hard. Every ounce of him wanted to pump the guy full of bullets, but Benjamin was right. His war was with Carlo. "Stand up. Today's your lucky day, but you're not getting off that easy." Walker handed Benjamin his gun, tightened his rage into a fist, and pummeled it into the man's temple. His target fell backwards over a table and onto the floor. "If I find out you did something to her, I will come back and kill you," Walker shouted.

"Feel better?" Benjamin asked, handing Walker back his pistol.

"Not much. Let's get her out of this hellhole." Walker holstered his gun and scooped Stacia's body into his arms like he had many times before. However, instead of throwing verbal barbs his way like she had the last time he insisted on carrying her to the destination of his choosing, her lifeless body didn't put up a fight. He followed Benjamin out of the office as a series of gunshots rang out. Benjamin stopped short at the top of the stairs holding his gun steady at a target at the bottom of the stairs.

"Drop the gun!"

Walker moved to Benjamin's side following his line of vision to the first floor where the man he recognized as Jake swayed the barrel of his gun in his direction. "It's over, Jake. Let us go without trouble and I'll make sure you don't see any jail time." Carlo was the one they wanted. Walker was sure he could arrange a plea bargain for the others.

"You think I'd turn on Carlo like Bruno did? That would leave me exactly where he is. Dead."

Walker's stare could've burned a hole into Jake's head when his thoughts moved to Potter and Nighthawk. He hoped they didn't pay the ultimate price during this mission. "What do you want?"

Jake jerked his head toward Walker. "Leave her and I'll let you walk out."

"Not a chance," Walker spat.

"You stole our latest shipment. She'll do until we can arrange for more trainees."

"Your *shipment* is now telling their story to the police. This whole operation is going down, and you're sinking with it, Jake. I handed you a 'Get Out of Jail Free' card. If you were smart you'd take it."

A moment of doubt glazed over Jake's face as he weighed his options. Walker knew they didn't have a second to spare so he forced Jake's answer. "Let's go," he said to Benjamin, who started down the stairs first.

"Stop!" Terror flashed in Jake's eyes as he pointed the gun up the stairs. "You screwed me over once. I'm not going to let you do it again. My life's over no matter what, so I choose to be a hero in the eyes of Carlo," Jake said, his quivering voice matching his hand as he aimed the gun at Walker.

Walker reached for his gun when the shot rang out. He swiveled his body to protect Stacia as he heard Benjamin bite out a string of swear words.

"Benjamin!" he called. Walker prayed the bullet didn't find his closest friend. Another gunshot sounded followed by a muffled thud at the bottom of the stairs. Walker pulled himself up with Stacia still in his arms and his gaze landed on Benjamin's shoulder. A deep red stain grew by the second. "You've been shot."

"No shit, boss," Benjamin said with a chuckle. "Looks worse than it is. It grazed me. Hardly feel a thing." He winced.

Walker's gaze traveled to the floor below and landed on Jake's crumpled body. Nighthawk appeared next to the trail of blood. "Carlo's reinforcements will be back. We have to get out now!"

Walker raced after Benjamin down the stairs and Nighthawk hustled them down the hallway toward the side door. "Where's Potter?" Walker asked fearing the worst.

"He's okay. He's outside with the girls." Nighthawk's face paled. "Is she…"

"I think she's drugged, but she's breathing. We have to get her to the hospital," Walker said as the older man's eyes welled with tears when his gaze washed over Stacia's pale face.

The door flew open and a dark form took up most of the doorway. It was another one of Carlo's soldiers. A flash of metal caught Walker's eye as the man extended his hand armed with a gun. "Carlo says the girl stays," he barked.

"I don't take orders from Carlo. I'd get out of here if I were you. The place will be crawling with cops in a few minutes." Benjamin, Nighthawk, Potter, and Walker had agreed not to involve the authorities until Stacia and the girls were out of the club. He figured Carlo would use them as hostages. However, they'd planned if five minutes passed without a word or signal, whoever was on the outside would make the call.

"Carlo says she's payment for his lost business. She stays."

Nighthawk pointed his pistol at the man's head. "She goes."

"Stupid old man," the guy spat and smashed Nighthawk on the side of his head with the gun. Nighthawk held onto his gun and managed to recover long enough to lodge a bullet into the man's temple before falling to the ground.

Walker bent next to him while holding Stacia. Blood seeped from the wound, staining Nighthawk's grey hair. "Benjamin, help him up. Let's get the hell out of here."

Benjamin moved to Nighthawk's side, but the older man waved him off. "Don't worry about me. Get her out of here."

"Not a chance. Walker's rule is no agent gets left behind," Benjamin said as he pulled Nighthawk to his feet. "Put your arm around me. We're leaving together."

Walker followed the men out as a chorus of sirens blared outside. Red lights blinked from the opened door, casting shadows around the carnage of a battle that had only begun. But winning the battle didn't matter anymore. The only thing that did was the woman in his arms. He pulled her closer to his chest. "Stay with me, Stacia. You can't leave me now. I love you." His voice rasped against her cheek.

Chapter Twenty-Two

Walker wore a path on the hospital's waiting room floor over the next few hours. Benjamin had been stitched up and his body pumped with fluids and antibiotics. As he suspected, the bullet grazed his left shoulder and he'd make a full recovery. Nighthawk was being admitted for a concussion, but he'd also be fine in a few days. Walker was relieved his men were okay, but he couldn't relax until he knew the condition of the girls and Stacia.

"Walker!"

He swung around as Howard Brodie, chief of the Las Vegas police force, moved toward him. "How are they?" Local law enforcement took custody of the dozen girls they'd rescued, now in the process of being examined and questioned.

"They're all pretty shaken up and they want to go home. Looks like a few were roughed up, but you got to them before anything serious happened."

Walker let out a breath. He couldn't forgive himself for not being there in time to help Stacia before they did whatever the hell they did to her. The wait to find out was killing him. He rubbed his eyes and leaned his hand against the wall.

"You look like shit, man."

"I feel like shit." Adrenaline drained from his body, and the impact of the day weighed on his shoulders.

"You should've involved us before you did. This isn't a you against the law thing, Walker. If we have any chance of destroying the Cardinellis we have to work together."

"I know how you guys work and how the Cardinellis operate. You'd show up with lights and sirens blaring and they'd shoot up those girls one at a time to prove a point. Sorry, Brodie, but my way was the only way." He'd had enough dealings with police forces in general to know how they'd react.

"That's bullshit. We've partnered with the Feds on mafia stings before and we'd be willing to work with you, too, but you need to be our partner, not our adversary. I don't like surprises."

Walker raised his eyebrow. "Okay. Here's the first step in the partnership: take me with you when you return the girls back to Mexico."

Chief Brodie narrowed his eyes. "Why would you want to do that? Hell, why would I let you do that? I'm sending a couple of my Spanish speaking female officers to escort them home. The sooner the better. My focus is to gather enough evidence to throw Carlo behind bars."

Walker shook his head. "Don't you get it? You're treating this like it's a one-time thing. Get your head out of your ass, Brodie. The Cardinellis have been doing this for years. Their clubs are filled with underage girls like the ones here. They send good-looking men to lure young girls with the promise of fame and fortune. Once they get them stateside, they funnel them into their clubs as sex slaves. He'll do it again here in Vegas. It's a matter of time. We need to get down there and cut Cardinelli off at the source. Last night's bust may have shut down operations at that club, but there is a fuck load more of them. Carlo will be more careful how he does it, but he'll continue if we let him. He needs to be stopped."

Chief Brodie screwed up his mouth like he was gnawing the inside of his cheek in deep thought. "Let's consider this my olive branch. No way in hell would I allow it normally, but in the spirit of partnership, I'll agree and I'll come along to make sure you stick to your word and don't go rogue on us."

Walker worked alone and it didn't sit well with him to work with the cops, but if it would save just one other girl from the Cardinellis it would be worth it. "When do we leave?"

"Don't know. We're in the process of securing approvals to charter a plane. It's not easy to navigate bureaucratic red tape."

"Exactly why I don't like to deal with you guys. I have a plane ready to go. Let me know when the girls are released. We'll go tonight."

Chief Brodie nodded slowly. "Thanks, Platinum. You're not as much of an asshole as I thought you were."

"Don't get mushy on me, Brodie. I'm still an asshole."

Chief Brodie clapped him on the back. "Your other guy wants to see you. He won't give us any information until he talks to you. He's a tough old bird."

"That's something we both agree on," Walker said, heading through the double doors into the ER.

"How many times do I have to tell you? Leave me alone!" Nighthawk's voice boomed through the hall.

A nurse whipped open the curtain. "Good luck with him," she grumbled as Walker stepped inside.

Walker hitched his thumb over his shoulder. "I see you're making friends."

Nighthawk pinned Walker with his stare. "How's Stacia? They won't tell me anything."

Walker dragged the lone chair to the bed side and sat, bringing him to eye level with the man. He suddenly felt as old as Nighthawk looked. "She's stable. I'm waiting to see her," Walker said, meeting his stare.

Nighthawk grunted. "She'll be okay?"

Walker rubbed his eyes. "Yeah, she'll be okay." Thank God it was the answer they both wanted to hear. It could've been worse. So much worse.

"She's all I have, Platinum."

"I know, and Carlo does, too. That's why she's in the middle of this. Why didn't you tell her about your involvement with Platinum? As far as she knew you spent your days playing cards at the senior citizen center."

"Because I worried this would happen," Nighthawk said, shaking his head. "But it did anyway. It was best she didn't know. It would put her in even more danger."

"More danger? Stacia just went through hell. She could've been killed. She could've been—" Walker stood, sending the chair banging against the wall. "How much more fucking danger could she have been in?"

Nighthawk groaned as he sat up. His eyes blazed at Walker. "You're looking to blame someone for this. I'll take responsibility for my daughter. I always have and always will, but have you always been honest with her? Did she know how much danger she was in?" he asked evenly. "Get it through your thick skull. It's *all* of our faults she's lying in a hospital bed right now. Yours, mine, and hers. She put herself in danger by defying you. You have no idea what you're dealing with."

Walker narrowed his eyes at Nighthawk as he sucked back a slew of profanity filled responses that stuck at the tip of his tongue because fuck, the man was right. He smashed his fist against the wall knocking a metal tray from the counter to the floor with a crash. The curtain whipped back revealing the same nurse Walker saw when he arrived. "This isn't a bar, gentlemen. Keep it down or I'll ask you to leave."

"I've been trying to leave since I got here," Nighthawk mumbled.

She raised her eyebrows. "Not you. Him," she said, pointing at Walker.

"I'm leaving. We'll talk later." He started toward the curtain.

"There won't be a later. As soon as I know Stacia's okay I'm going home. This place gives me the shakes."

"Don't be an idiot. It's not safe for you to go home, and you know it. There were cameras all over the club. He knows you were part of it, and there will be a price on your head. You have to come back to New Orleans with us, at least until we have a plan."

"And live like a caged animal? I'd rather die. It won't be the first time someone's wanted me dead."

"It doesn't take a genius to figure out where Stacia gets her pig-headedness from," Walker said.

Nighthawk chuckled. "She has an extra dose of it. Her mother was worse than me." He tilted his head, and his eyes softened. "You love my daughter, don't you?"

"Is it that obvious?" For someone who lived his life keeping his emotions in check, Walker certainly wore his heart on his sleeve when it came to Stacia.

"I may be old, but I'm not dead. Look, I can take care of myself, but there's something you can do for me."

Walker crossed his arms. "What's that, General?"

"Take care of Stacia. Get her underground with zero outside contact, at least until you figure out Cardinelli's next move. And you must earn her trust and make her earn yours."

"Keep her locked up but earn her trust." Walker shook his head. If only it was that easy. "That's impossible."

"If anyone can do it, you can. I have faith in you, Walker."

Walker nodded and extended his hand. "It's been an honor to meet you in person, sir."

Nighthawk returned his handshake. "If there's anyone who can take down the Cardinellis, it's you and Stacia." He paused for a moment. "Together."

The curtain whisked open and a woman in scrubs Walker recognized her as one of the doctors who'd attended to Stacia as soon as she was brought in on the ambulance gurney strode to the bed. "General Howell, Mr. Platinum? I'm Dr. Roth, I've been treating Stacia since she was brought in." She turned toward Nighthawk. "Is it okay to talk freely about Stacia's condition with Mr. Walker?"

Nighthawk nodded his agreement.

"Would you like to sit?" Dr. Roth gestured to two chairs a couple feet away from the bed. Walker was suddenly so exhausted he could hardly keep his eyes open. He followed Dr. Roth and took a seat. "As you suspected, Stacia was drugged. I gave her something to counteract the effects, and she's starting to come out of it."

Walker tipped his head back against the wall. "Thank God," he muttered.

"I don't know how much divine intervention had to do with it, but it's a good thing you found her when you did. The drugs in her system not only render a person helplessly unconscious, it also slows the person's breathing. She could've suffocated with her mouth taped. You saved her life."

"She'll be okay?" he asked.

"I'm confident she'll make a full recovery. Her vitals are strong. It'll take some time for the drug to work its way out of her system, but she should regain consciousness soon."

"Was she ... did they..." Walker was never at loss for words, but he couldn't bring himself to ask the question that had rolled around in his head since the moment he pulled that asshole off her body.

She shook her head. "There's no evidence of rape. No broken bones or bruising. And even though she'd had a few doses of flunitrazepam, it wasn't enough to cause any residual effects. She was lucky."

He savored the first few words. No evidence of rape. She wasn't hurt. Walker felt like an Army tank had slid from his shoulders. He'd spend the rest of his days making sure Stacia was safe.

"Would you like to see her? We can get a wheelchair for General Howell." The doctor's voice brought him back to the present.

"You go ahead, Walker. I'll visit with her later," Nighthawk said, his eyes offering an unspoken pact. *Take care of Stacia.*

Walker ran his hand over his stubbled face and nodded. He followed Dr. Roth to the nurses' station where she waved Walker in as she stopped to speak to another doctor. His gaze landed on Stacia when he stepped into her room. A cloud of dark hair fell over the stark white pillow. Tubes ran up her nose and into her arm as she lay completely still. Walker dragged a chair to her bedside. He tucked a lock of hair behind her ear, his chest feeling like it might crack open as he searched her face for signs of the Stacia he loved. She was there, inside the hazy mask of Cardinelli filth. Their actions on Stacia were a direct attack on him. Thank God they didn't do the unthinkable. Walker wouldn't be able to bear it. He'd give up his own life to avenge Stacia. His gaze trailed down her blanket covered form and watched her chest rhythmically rise and fall next to her arm that lay bare on the bed, as fluids were being pumped into her body.

He laced his fingers with hers and squeezed gently, hoping she'd know he was there through the fog she was fighting to conquer. "I'm so sorry I got you wrapped up in all this, Princess. But now that you are, there's no turning back. I will personally see to it that you are never harmed again. Whatever it takes, I will protect and love you. Always." He leaned over and pressed a light kiss on her forehead. He thought he'd felt her fingers move as he pulled his hand away. Walker sat in silence for a few minutes getting lost in the sound of her breath before he pulled his phone from his pocket and tapped the screen. "Potter. I need you at the hospital to stand outside Stacia's room. No one goes inside unless they're a doctor or nurse with a hospital ID. I'm going to Mexico, but I want you to text me updates hourly, unless something happens, then I want to know immediately."

He ended the call and stood, his eyes still locked on Stacia. She had no idea how much her life was about to change. They had no choice. He made a promise to himself and to Nighthawk. She was his and his alone.

Chapter Twenty-Three

Lifting her heavy lids, Stacia squinted through the bright light. A fleeting thought crossed her mind that perhaps she were dead, but her pounding headache chased it away. Death wouldn't hurt so much. "Walker?" She barely recognized her own words.

A calloused hand covered hers. "It's okay. Don't try to talk."

She closed her eyes, falling into the safety of her father's presence. "Dad." She turned toward his voice, her eyes fluttering open, but everything was out of focus. "Where are we?"

"The hospital."

"Walker? Is he…"

"He's okay. Everyone's okay." His rough thumb slid over the back of her hand.

She swallowed. Her throat felt like it was lined with broken glass. "Water?"

"Of course. Here."

A motor sounded as her back rose. She blinked again, and her father's bandaged face came into view. "What happened?"

He held a plastic cup and angled the straw to her mouth. "Drink."

Cold water coated her throat. She took the cup from her father and took another sip. "Thanks. Now please explain what's going on."

He took her through an abbreviated version of what had happened after Stacia was taken from the bookstore. She was relieved to learn Leena and the other girls were safe and that Walker was personally seeing them home to their families. "When I left the house that day, I had no idea what kind of danger I was in and then put you in. I'm sorry."

"Walker thought he was protecting you."

"He was so distant. He wouldn't tell me anything. He barely spoke to me after he found out you were my father. I thought we had … I don't know … something, but then he went back to treating me like a stranger, like he didn't trust me," she said as the event of the past few days weighed heavy on her head.

"Stacia, you have to understand men like Walker are trained to keep things close to their chest. He divulges information on a need to know basis. Not because he doesn't trust you, because he's trying to keep you safe."

"Hold on." She remembered something Carlo told her in his office. "Is Walker really Mark Platinum? Is his identity another thing I didn't need to know?"

"I wish he could've told you first, but yes. Walker is Mark Platinum. He keeps his identity a secret for obvious reasons."

"Carlo knows it. Carlo seems to know a lot. How?"

Her father shook his head, and for the first time he looked like an old man to Stacia. Her father was always bigger than life. Sitting next to her in bandages, he appeared frail and delicate. "We're not sure. Platinum has the top security and surveillance technology, but the Cardinellis' intel always seems to be a step ahead. We can't seem to stop it."

She rubbed her eyes. "So many secrets. Why didn't you tell me about being a Platinum agent?"

He patted her hand. "When your mother died, you were the only important thing I had. You still are. I thought by staying undercover, I could work for Platinum anonymously. It was like being invisible. But Carlo figured it out somehow, and he found you. So I didn't do such a great job protecting you after all."

She shook her head. "That's not true. You did what you thought was right. I'm able to take care of myself."

"Stacia, four men risked their lives to save you yesterday. You may have been able to take care of yourself before you got wrapped up in Platinum and the Cardinellis. Your life is different now. You're in the middle of a strategic game, and you either become a player or—" His eyes were full of concern as they bored into hers. "Well, you have to become a player. You have no choice."

"So now my life is supposed to be spent running from Carlo?"

"Not at all. I didn't raise you to run from anyone. You're a Howell. You need to help take down Carlo with Walker."

"With Walker," she repeated. "Dad, Walker is moody, uncooperative, unreasonable, and … and…"

"And in love with you," he interrupted. "And you're in love with him."

She couldn't hold back her smile.

Her father winked. "He needs you as much as you need him."

"But is he ever going to really let me inside that hard head of his?"

He chuckled again. "Funny, he said something similar about you." He intertwined his fingers with hers. "I know I was hard on you growing up, but I've always loved you. You know that, don't you?"

Tears stung her eyes. She always felt his love, but it was the first time he'd actually spoken the words. She could only nod.

"You two can take the Cardinellis down. I know you can. I only hope I live long enough to see it happen."

She gripped his hand. "Why would you say that,

Dad?"

"No reason. Just an old man's rambles. Just promise me you won't give up on him. You can do great things, Stacia. You're my daughter. You can do anything you put your mind to, and with Walker you'll be unstoppable."

Chapter Twenty-Four

One week later

Stacia rolled her roped wrists in circles and wondered how much longer she'd have to wait. Wasn't it enough to have been stuck in the house for a week with no access to the outside world? Benjamin had even disabled the cable and internet services and wouldn't give her any information. He would only say it was Walker's orders. Well, Walker had made his point. She knew he was furious with her for going against his wishes and leaving the house the day she was kidnapped. His demand that she assumed the submissive position on her knees with her chest to the floor spoke volumes. He was going to punish her, and truth was, she wanted it. She craved it. But she was also angry with him for leaving her alone and she had her own payback plan.

She lifted her ass from her heels and tried to shake the pins and needles from her left foot when her ears perked at the familiar sound of footsteps ascending the Tower Room staircase. Heavy footfalls crept closer until they stopped at her back. She inhaled a deep breath, picking up the notes of Walker's musky scent.

"Nice of you to show up, Walker. Or should I call you Mark now?" she asked, turning her head to see his reaction. If he was surprised, he didn't show it.

"My name is and always has been Walker. I never lied to you about my name. My given name is Mark Walker Platinum, and I do regret not telling you sooner who I am. Okay?"

"Wow. An almost apology."

"I don't have to remind you to keep your eyes to the ground," he said evenly.

She whipped her head back and trained her eyes to a spot on the floor.

"Seems the only way to keep you in one place is to tie you up, Princess." A swoosh of his pants filled her ears and a pair of scuffed black boots came into view. "Look at me."

Her gaze first hit the bulge in his well-worn jeans. She swallowed hard as her eyes tracked to the dark line of hair under his bellybutton and lingered over this view of Walker she'd never seen, the unhinged, wild version. As her gaze continued to his face, she noticed what looked to be a few days of stubbled growth on his jawline. She hesitated before meeting his stare. A pang of regret rang through her chest when she took in the deep lines etching his eyes. *Her* actions created this version of Walker. The Walker she'd known never had a hair out of place or even a five o'clock shadow. He was livid, and Stacia knew she'd pay for it. She was about to find out how.

"I've been here for a week with no word from you." She figured she was walking a thin line, but she was also pissed and she wanted answers.

"I was in Mexico, returning the girls to their families and looking for anything to help stop Carlo from doing it again."

"What happened there?" she asked in barely a whisper.

Walker's gaze seared through her before he reached to her face and smoothed the hair away that had fallen over her eye. "Now's not the time. I'll tell you everything but not now."

"I need to know."

"You do and you will."

"What do you want from me, Walker? An apology for leaving without you that day? I said I was sorry, but you weren't fucking here to accept it. What else do you want?" She searched his eyes.

"You still have no idea of the impact of your actions."

"I get it, but my actions ended up saving all of those young girls. If I didn't get kidnapped and brought to the club, Carlo and those dirty fucks would've done horrible things to them."

"I'll give you that, but you can't ignore what you sacrificed. The safety of my men, including your own father."

"I know, and I'm sorry." Her eyes burned as she swallowed a sob.

He glared at her and ran his hand through his hair as he eyed her tied wrists. "Others risked their lives to save you. Benjamin for example. I trust he took good care of you while I was gone."

"He did."

"Did he also tell you he was shot in the shoulder that night while saving you?"

Her breath stuck in her throat. "He didn't tell me."

"Didn't think so. Benjamin is a professional. He'll do anything I ask him to do without question." He stepped back and his gaze trailed down her body. "He brought you here and secured your wrists. How do you feel about him seeing you like this?"

"It was uncomfortable, if you want to know the truth."

"You don't like feeling that way?"

"Fuck, no. Would you?" she spat.

His eyes bored through her, but she refused to be the one to look away. "You thought that was uncomfortable? Brace yourself, Princess." She detected a moment of hesitation before he turned away and walked toward the door. Was he leaving? *What the fuck?* Male voices murmured behind her before two sets of footsteps headed her way. "On your feet," his voice boomed.

She scrambled to stand but stumbled when she put weight on her half-asleep extremity. The heat of Walker's body ghosted behind her as he held her hips while she shored her footing. A motor sounded from above her head and her wrists were pulled upward so that her hands were straight over her head. She turned toward the row of switches on the wall to find Benjamin in control of the retracting cord.

Walker stepped around until he faced her and Benjamin strode to his side holding a small metal bowl.

"I asked Benjamin to join us," Walker said as if he was including him in their lunch plans. "You don't mind, do you?"

Her mouth flew open, and her gaze bounced from Walker to Benjamin and back to Walker. Was he serious?

"No spewing swear words? No smart-ass remark? That's a first, Princess. Since she's at a loss of words, why don't you break the ice and explain to Ms. Howell what you did to save her life at The Silver Club."

Benjamin nodded. "I hacked into the club's security system, immobilized a guard, kicked down a few doors, and I was shot as we left. Bullet grazed my shoulder."

"You broke several laws, risked your life, and were shot to get her out of the building?" Walker asked.

"Yes. That sums it up."

"Tell Ms. Howell why you did these things."

"Because they were my orders."

"Do you ever question my orders, Benjamin?"

"Never," he answered.

"Why is that?"

"Because I trust you implicitly. If you require me to do something there's a good reason for it even if it's not immediately apparent."

"Remove Ms. Howell's top, Benjamin."

Benjamin face whipped in Walker's direction. Walker confirmed with a curt nod before Benjamin placed the bowl on the floor, stepped forward, and untied the bow between her breasts. The material grazed over her sensitive nipples as he pulled the ends of the ribbon from each eyelet. Cool air hit her skin damp with perspiration when Benjamin loosened the garment enough for it to fall from her torso and land with a soft thud at her feet. Benjamin retrieved the corset and moved to return to his spot next to Walker.

"Stay where you are, Benjamin." Walker exchanged the corset in Benjamin's hand with the bowl.

Stacia's gaze fell to the bowl's contents, and she narrowed her eyes.

"Are you still feeling uncomfortable, Princess?"

Her heart beat wildly. "Yes. And even more so by the second."

"Good, because we've just started."

Her eyes widened, and she craned her neck around Benjamin to find Walker. She opened her mouth.

"Unless you are going to safeword out, you are not to speak. Understood?"

She closed her mouth and nodded. *Red.* She brought the word to the front of her mind as a reminder it was her way out. One word would stop it all. But where would it leave her? She obviously couldn't return to her old life, the one without Tower Rooms or restraints or Mark "Walker" Platinum. Even if she wanted to, which she was sure would be impossible considering the current landscape with the Cardinellis. She couldn't imagine returning to that world after sampling Walker's life. Experiencing Walker was like sipping a fine wine for the first time. Once tasted, everything else paled in comparison.

"Ms. Howell has beautiful tits, doesn't she, Benjamin?"

"Gorgeous, sir."

"So fucking responsive, too." Walker stuck his hand in the bowl and pulled out an ice cube. Holding the cube between his thumb and index finger, he held it against her collarbone until a slow drip trailed over her breast and she groaned softly. "It's your turn," Walker said to Benjamin as he nodded to the bowl.

The tinkling of ice filled her ears as Benjamin lifted one from the bowl and set the container on the floor. Stacia caught the look Benjamin shot Walker's way as if he was ensuring he understood Walker's directive. Walker closed his eyes for a moment before nodding once.

"Relax. I won't hurt you," Benjamin whispered before he cupped the side of Stacia's face with his free hand and tipped her head upward. Her breath caught when a cold sensation hit the flesh below her ear and slowly traveled down her neck and over her collarbone. He repeated the motion on the other side, but this time he continued dragging the cube to the middle of her chest before he flattened the ice between his palm and her heated skin. Water dripped down her belly as her gaze landed on Walker.

"Continue," he said.

Benjamin hesitated for a half-second before he bent and the rattle of cubes echoed in her head as he retrieved another from the bowl. She flinched when the frozen object hit the curve of her waist and continued up her ribs. She closed her eyes when he drew a wet line over her breast and made wide circles around her nipple. She held her breath as the circles became tighter and faster.

"Open your eyes, Princess. I want you to watch what Benjamin's doing to you."

She swallowed hard and opened her eyes. Her gaze landed on Benjamin's glistening fingers and dripping ice cube grazing over her erect nipple. A moan escaped from her lips at the image. Benjamin blew a warm breath over her breast before following the ice trail with his tongue. Her legs weakened from the overload of senses. Wet heat of his mouth over her flesh mingled with the numbing ice, sending her to an undiscovered level of pleasure. She pressed her legs together as her clit tingled in anticipation. Walker strode to her back and nudged her legs open.

"I decide when you come and it won't be anytime soon." His voice rumbled in her ears.

She whimpered as Benjamin moved to her other breast. Each stroke of his tongue and rotation of the cube sent pulses to her sex. Every nerve ending in her body stood at attention. A ragged breath left her mouth as waves of need raged over her pussy. She was at the edge of climax without a single stroke below the waist.

"Stop," Walker said.

Benjamin halted his actions and dropped the remaining nub of ice in the bowl next to his feet. Stacia sucked in a breath as Benjamin stepped back waiting for his next order. She bit her lip to hold back a slew of obscenities on the tip of her lips. Her pussy throbbed with need. If he'd only…

"Walker, please." She closed her eyes and cursed the weakness in her voice.

Walker ignored her plea. Her picked up the bowl and handed it to Benjamin. "That will be all tonight. You're free to take the rest of the evening off. I've contacted Madame Lucene and ensured Victoria will be free this evening."

Benjamin nodded. "Thank you." His gaze tipped to Stacia for a split second before leaving.

A shiver ran through her body as she came off the high. It was as if she were traveling at high speed toward a cliff and stopped suddenly before falling over the side. She rolled her wrists in the rope, which suddenly felt tight, and the residual beads of water chilled her skin. Walker flipped the switch on the wall releasing the rope holding her hands. Was that it? Did she fail Walker's kink test?

Without a word, he untied her hands and rubbed her wrists between his palms. She hadn't noticed the robe draped over his arm which he held open while she slipped her arms through the sleeves.

"Are we … done?" she asked.

A crooked smile played at his lips. "Why? Do you have somewhere you need to be?"

"Well, no, but…" She shook her head. A jumble of emotions fought for attention in her head.

"Take a deep breath, Princess. We're just getting started, but you need a break. It was a lot of stimulation."

She relaxed as her body warmed under the robe. Walker gestured toward the bed. "Sit. I'll get you something to drink."

Stacia drew her legs under her and leaned back against the headboard hoping he'd return with a large glass of wine. Instead he handed her a steaming mug of herbal tea. She took a sip and let the hot liquid chase the chill from her body. "You surprise me," she said quietly.

The mattress dipped as he sat on the edge. "Care to elaborate?"

The steam warmed her face as she held the mug between her hands. "I never took you as the sharing type."

"I don't share. What happened was necessary to

prove a point. If you're going to be in my inner circle, you need to earn it. I must trust when I tell you to do something it will be done. Just like Benjamin. He doesn't question any of my requests."

Her heart fluttered. He wanted her in his inner circle? "So that sort of thing doesn't happen all the time?"

"Never has and it will never again. When it comes to you, I've found myself doing many things I never thought I would. I need to know it's worth it."

Suddenly everything clicked. He didn't want to punish her out of hatred. This was a test. One that she'd have to decide if she was willing to take. The reward for passing was Walker. She handed him the mug and loosened the robe's sash. The fabric fell off her shoulders, and her body warmed as his gaze moved to her breasts. "Show me what it takes to earn your trust."

Chapter Twenty-Five

Stacia lay naked on her stomach as instructed. She lost track of how long Walker had left her in that position. Was it a few minutes or close to an hour? Time seemed to stop in the Tower Room. The regular world and everyone in it also ceased to exist. Nothing mattered while she was a guest in the room. Even though it was devoid of windows and the sparse furnishings were imposing and impersonal, she'd felt safe inside, as though she belonged. It was a sensation she'd rarely experienced in her life. Growing up, she'd never lived in the same place long enough to plant roots of any kind. She'd always been a visitor in other people's worlds. But there, in a room built for pain and pleasure with a man who was so hard to reach, she was complete. How fucked up was that?

A soft click echoed in the room followed by a deep beat that filled her ears and vibrated in her chest. She closed her eyes, allowing the music to calm her nerves and clear her head. She stretched her legs and arched her back, contracting her muscles and letting them relax. Deep breaths floated in through her nose and out her mouth. Walker appeared at her side with a tray in his hands. He set it on the mattress and her eyes locked on the contents. A half dozen lit candles in glass holders flickered. Her gaze moved to what looked like a black ball connected to a buckled strap on the tray. Thanks to her research, she knew exactly what it was for. "You're going to gag me?" she asked and sat up.

"Then you've seen one of these before." He picked up a remote and tapped a button lowering the music's volume.

"Yeah. It's a ball gag. I don't know about this." Her heart beat an uneven rhythm.

"It wasn't on your list of hard limits. If you don't want it just say the word."

Her gaze flicked back to the ball. What the hell was wrong with her? She'd been tied up, blindfolded, flogged, iced and fondled by a third party. But she'd always had the power to say one word to bring everything to a halt. "What if I can't handle it? What do I do if I want to stop?"

"Simple. You're going to hold these." He held two ping-pong balls in his palm. "Dropping the balls is the same as saying red. Everything stops and the gag comes off when the balls hit the floor."

She searched the tray again. "What's with the candles?"

Walker picked up a glass holder and held the flame between them. He tipped it slightly and the clear liquid pooled at the side of the glass. "The best part. They're special candles made with massage oil. Not as hot as a wax candle." He tilted his head. "What do you think? If you're out, say so."

Stacia wet her lips and stared at the flame. She was in. So very in. She scooped the ping-pong balls from his hand and nodded.

Fire burned in Walker's eyes and caused her chest to swell with pride. She never thought she'd get so much happiness from pleasing a man, but there she was waiting to be gagged and bound by the only man she'd ever trust enough to put her in that situation. The man she loved. He raised the volume before three velvet strips appeared from his pocket and he secured her wrists on either side of the headboard. Walker gathered her hair into a ponytail and used the third piece to hold it into place. Finally, he pinched either end of the gag straps between his thumb and index finger and lifted the ball from the tray. "Open up, Princess."

Her eyes were trained on his face as he slid the ball into place behind her teeth. The leather straps popped and cracked as he stretched them around her head and tightened the buckle. Stacia pulled air through her nose and the scent of rubber comingled with the essence of cedar wood and pomegranate of the candle. Counting to three on each inhale and exhale, she steadied her breath, chasing the anxiety from her body.

"Doing okay?" he asked.

She nodded as a calm wave settled over her body and she rolled the balls in her hand. She could do this.

His gaze never left her face. "You're so beautiful like this." A hiss sent her gaze to the side as Walker lifted one of the candles. A pool of glistening oil floated under the golden flame. "I'm using massage oil candles instead of wax for your first time. They're not as hot and easier to remove from your skin." He tipped a few drops onto her forearm and she ground her teeth on the ball. Not as hot, her ass. The gag prevented her from dropping a few choice obscenities, which would've earned her more punishment. But after the first sting, her flesh buzzed and she wanted more. He continued dripping hot oil up her arm, between her breasts and down the center of her chest to her belly button. She watched as some of the drops pooled on her skin while others formed an oily trail over her abdomen and dripped onto the mattress. She stared at his hand as he meticulously decorated her skin with oil. Stacia bucked her hips as he shifted lower and knelt between her legs. A steady tempo of drops fell over her heated sex as he coaxed her legs further apart with his knees. Tears blurred her vision, and her jaw ached as the warm oil dripped over her clit. She willed his hand to follow the trail of oil. One touch would send her spiraling deep into climax. As though he read her mind he traced one of the oily lines on her inner thigh with his fingertip.

"It's agony being so close to something you want but it being out of reach. It's how I felt when I couldn't get to you." The dripping continued faster on her clit and oil coated her aching folds. She dug her heels into the mattress and curled her toes. One touch was all she needed. *One. Touch.*

A groan she hardly recognized as her own started low in her throat. She yanked at the restraints before the click of something hitting the floor sounded in both ears. It took her a moment to figure out what had made the sounds. The ping-pong balls. In her agony, she'd let go of the balls. In a blur, Walker had pulled off the gag and released her hands. *Game over.*

"No. I didn't mean to. Please." A jumble of words fell from her lips as he gathered her into his lap.

His strong hands rubbed her wrists and continued slowly up her forearms. "It's okay. Lay back, Princess. I'll take care of you," he whispered.

Closing her eyes, she relaxed her back against his chest as his fingers trailed to her oil coated breasts. His fingers gleamed as he coaxed her nipples into tightened peaks. Her heart kicked into overdrive as he flattened his palms along her ribcage and slid them toward her belly. She'd been slipping on the edge of climax for so long and it'd take a few strokes of his hand to send her over the cliff. As much as she wanted it, she wanted something else even more.

Stacia's oil slick hands tentatively encircled Walker's forearms. His muscles tensed under her touch, but he didn't move. She nuzzled her head into his chest, listening to his heartbeat as she laced her fingers with his.

"Stacia," he said huskily.

She turned and straddled his lap while guiding his hands to her hips.

His eyes blazed through her as he tightened his grip and pushed her weight on his steely erection. His throat worked down a swallow. She'd cracked his hard as nails exterior, the first step in claiming her prize. She ran her hands up her sides and slowly caressed her breasts, coating her palms with oil before flattening them on his chest. He pulled back as though her touch seared his flesh, but she continued working her fingers over his pecs and shoulders. In one quick swoop, he grabbed her wrists in one hand and her chin in the other.

"Don't," he growled. Puffs of angry breath blew hot on her mouth.

She locked his stare. To hell with him if he thought he'd scare her into submission. "It can't be one-sided. If you won't make love to me this isn't going to happen."

"That's what you want? To fuck?"

She shook her head. "I want more."

"I can't give you more."

"I think you can. I know you can."

"God damn it, Stacia." He pulled her off him and dropped her on the mattress. She figured he was heading out of the Tower Room. Out of the house. And ultimately, out of her life. But instead he moved to the cabinet and pulled open drawers two at a time until he found a foil square from one of the drawers and slammed the cabinet doors closed. He shucked his pants off within the two strides back to the bed. If he could throw daggers from his eyes, Stacia would've been speared to the mattress.

She should've been frightened, but she wasn't. Instead all she could see was his chest rising up and down, his bulging muscles, and finally his huge cock jutting out from a smattering of pubic hair. One thing came to mind. He was going to be hers and hers alone.

"Don't look so pleased with yourself, Princess."
He sat on the edge of the bed, ripped the package, and
rolled on the condom. He grabbed her waist with one
hand and held his shaft in the other as he pulled her down
onto his cock. There was no testing his size or letting her
get used to his girth. His action spoke volumes. If she
wanted him, she'd have him as he was: raw and
unapologetic.

She wouldn't have him any other way. He
wrapped her hair around his fist and pulled hard. She
cried out as he thrust into her core again. His breath was
hot on her forehead as she took him deeper into her body.
She raked her fingers through his sweat-soaked hair as he
lifted her body from the bed with his cock inside her.
Backing her against the wall, he hitched her bent knee
over one arm as he pummeled her body. He grabbed the
flesh of her backside and his thumb, slick with oil,
circled her puckered opening as the friction of his rhythm
teased her clit. "This is what it's like with me," he
ground out between thrusts.

"I never expected anything different," she said
breathlessly. She moaned in pleasure as her orgasm
climbed to the top of the dangerous cliff known as Mark
Walker Platinum. She'd take everything he'd had to give
her and savor it like a rare gift. His body began to shake
as his cock pulsed sending her over the edge into her own
climax. His movements slowed to a halt and they stayed
tangled together for a few moments as their breath
steadied together.

He tipped his forehead to hers and tucked a lock
of hair behind her ear. "What is it with you? You walked
into my life and turned it upside down." His breath was
warm on her lips.

She smiled. "I believe you carried me into your
life. I broke a heel, remember?"

"I can't lose you. I won't. But I need to know you're completely in. All the way."

"I am, but I need to know that you are, too."

"I love you, Stacia. I promise I'll protect you over everything. You'll always be safe with me."

She cupped each hand over his shoulders and gazed into his eyes. "I love you, too," she whispered.

When he finally set her down on her feet the fleeting visit into Walker's soul was over. He discarded his condom, retrieved her robe and slipped it over her shoulders before stepping into the next room. She was afraid to move and listened for footsteps heading down the staircase. The only sound she heard was running water before he returned with a washcloth in one hand and a towel in the other. Without a word, he washed the oil from her flesh until she was warm and dry. He tied the sash of her robe and pulled his jeans on without bothering with the button. With his hand at the small of her back, he guided her downstairs to her bedroom before tilting his head and pressing a light kiss to her lips.

She searched his eyes locking in on the intimacy they'd shared.

"Good night, Princess."

Stacia was about to protest, but the look in his eyes stopped her but not because he was angry. His eyes carried a different look altogether. One that she'd never seen on his face before. She was sure she'd pushed him so far out of his comfort zone, he needed time to reflect, and readjust. He'd thrown down the gauntlet and she picked it up and shown him she was up to the challenge.

The question was, could he truly let her in?

Chapter Twenty-Six

Walker was up before sunrise, which wasn't out of the ordinary. What was different was the lightness that floated through his body. He was almost happy. He even caught himself humming in the shower. Fucking humming. What the hell? He was supposed to meet Benjamin in the kitchen to strategize their next move with the Cardinellis, but he certainly couldn't let Benjamin see him in that condition. He needed to focus. He threw on a pair of shorts and a t-shirt and headed out the front door avoiding the kitchen. His feet hit the pavement of the quiet street. Few people were up and out at that hour, so Walker chose to run down the middle of Prytania Road, passing the cemetery toward the river. His calves started to burn after the first mile and he picked up his speed. The first rays of sunlight cast fuzzy shadows along the street followed by a rise in temperature. Sweat dripped into his eyes, and he pulled his shirt off and wiped his face with the material. The humid morning air coated his throat and made him wish he'd brought a bottle of cold water, but that would've required him to enter the kitchen where he'd have to answer a slew of questions from Benjamin at best, or Benjamin would pretend last night never happened, which would be worse. Walker would have to let Benjamin know what was going on in his head, but he had to make sense of it first.

He'd lived almost forty years without allowing a woman under his skin. His relationships—if he'd even call them that, they were more like arrangements—were one and done. He'd give and take what was needed and moved on. It worked well, until Stacia. The only thing that was clear to him after last night, was she belonged to him and he'd never let her go. His cock stirred at the thought of last night's power play. Stacia Howell was about to make his life a lot more interesting.

He slung the t-shirt around his neck and headed back. The sun beat hot on his shoulders, and he stuck to the sidewalks since the Garden District began to wake. Gardeners mowed and watered plants behind tall fences, residents left their homes for work, and children trudged to bus stops. Out of habit, Walker made a few turns and checked to see if he was being followed. He fully expected revenge from the Cardinellis. However, he also knew Carlo didn't react immediately. He was known for his calculated plans.

Walker used an access card to let himself into the garden where he found Benjamin and Stacia.

Stacia wore a pair of extremely short shorts showcasing her mile-high legs. The sleeves of her flowy blouse bunched when she crossed her arms. "Nice of you to tell someone where you were going."

"I figured Benjamin would know I went for a run."

"Yes, sir." Benjamin said and tossed him a bottle of water. Leave it to Benjamin to anticipate Walker's next step.

"He said that's where you were. At least Benjamin and I had a chance to talk about the awkwardness of last night." Stacia tipped her head in Benjamin's direction.

"Did you?" Walker asked.

"And we decided what's a little awkwardness between friends, right, Ben?" She nudged Benjamin and turned toward the house. "I know you two have things to discuss so I'll fix breakfast."

Walker waited until she shut the door behind her. "Ben?"

"I don't want to upset her by telling her I hate the

short version of my name."

"You two talked about last night?"

"I told her it was a test she passed with flying colors. It was just that, a test, I presume." Benjamin raised his eyebrows.

"You can be sure I'll never share Stacia with anyone ever again. It was necessary to prove a point."

"That's what I told her."

"I trust you had a good night?"

"Victoria was very accommodating. Thank you for arranging it."

"The least I could do." Walker took a seat on the outdoor sofa and leaned his elbows on his knees rolling the bottle between his hands. "Any word from the Cardinellis?"

"It's been quiet. Too quiet."

Benjamin nodded. "They're going to want to hit us hard and where it hurts. They're going to target Stacia. You know that."

Walker had an uneasy feeling in his gut. "They can't touch what's out of reach." His gaze traveled to the kitchen window.

"She mentioned calling her boss today to see if she can do some remote editing work for now."

"She can't have any outside communication until we know Carlo's next move. Did you tell her it was too dangerous?" Walker asked, watching her bounce around the kitchen. She must've turned on one of her dance music channels.

Benjamin slapped Walker on the back. "And deal with the fiery wrath of Stacia Howell? That honor is all yours."

Walker grunted, and his stomach rumbled. "Shower and breakfast first. I'd rather eat whatever she's making in there than wear it." He pointed to the phone in

Benjamin's hand. "Try Nighthawk again."

It had been a couple days since they'd talked. Nighthawk had gone back to his home in Cleveland and Walker had sent Potter to help him install more security and update his safe room. Nighthawk's home now had much of the same security technology as Prytania House.

Benjamin tapped the screen and held the phone to his ear for a moment. "It's going to voice mail."

Walker held his palm out, and Benjamin handed him the phone. "Nighthawk. It's Platinum. Get back to me when you get this." He gave the phone back to Benjamin and stared up at the sky. The sun was peeking over the roofline and about to spill bright rays over the brick patio. It would've been the perfect day to take Stacia on a motorcycle ride, but small luxuries like that were something he couldn't chance. Not now. Carlo and his top men had gone so far underground after the incident, no one had seen or heard from them since. None of Walker's informants had any information, and without Nighthawk's check-in, he was missing a universal piece of his intel. It was like working in the dark.

"Send Potter back to check on him." Walker didn't like the feeling needling through his belly like a worm. Maybe he was just on guard because he knew Cardinelli would resurface and he'd be out for revenge. Add in the connection with Stacia and the stakes quadrupled. He wished he'd insisted Nighthawk returned with them to Prytania House until Carlo dealt his next card.

Chapter Twenty-Seven

Walker entered the kitchen as she placed a platter of French toast on the table. His still damp hair looked almost black against his olive complexion and white button-down shirt, which was open at his chest. Stacia speared two slices with a fork and dropped them on Benjamin's plate before serving Walker and herself. She folded her hands together and stared at Walker, ready for battle. "I need to get back to work."

He shook his head. "Not happening."

"You can't keep pushing me off. Why are we sitting around waiting for Carlo to regroup? Let's expose Carlo for who he is. I can blow the story wide open and report on the Cardinelli human trafficking racket. It will stop him in his tracks and get him behind bars where he belongs."

"Don't you think that's what I want? It's not that easy. As soon as it becomes public, he'll destroy all evidence linking him to any of it. That means people will die, Stacia. The girls he's already smuggled in will die. He'll do anything to stay out of jail. Believe me, I've trying to take him down for a long time, and I won't give up until I do."

"Damn it, Walker. Why won't you let me help you?" she asked.

"I know it seems like nothing's happening, but you have to be patient. Dealing with Carlo is like a game of chess. We have to wait for his next move."

For one of the first times in her life, she felt helpless. Her chest ached as her world spun out of control. "For how long?"

He shook his head. Silence filled the space around them.

"Walker?"

His gaze moved to hers. "Don't you get it? From this point forward, your life will never be the same. You've seen firsthand what Carlo is capable of, and what you witnessed that night was only the beginning. I was in Mexico last week to help take the girls home and back to their families, and I found out as we suspected, that wasn't the first time he'd stolen young girls from Nogales. He's been doing it for years, and he'll do it again. The Cardinellis are like cockroaches. They'll go underground and come back stronger than ever. We will destroy him and the entire Cardinelli organization my way, and that doesn't include you broadcasting our intel."

"So what now? I get locked in your fucking castle like some damsel in distress? I'm not a fucking princess, Walker. Whether you want me to be or not." She cursed her shaky voice.

"I know." He pulled her into his chest. "But you're who they want because they know the only chance they have of destroying me is through you. Carlo thinks you're my weakness, but don't you see? You're my strength. I'm not letting you go." He palmed the back of her neck and lowered his face to hers. He brushed his lips along her mouth once.

She wrapped her arms around his neck and the tension rolled off her shoulders as he claimed her mouth. His tongue caressed her bottom lip before coaxing her mouth open. Standing on her tiptoes, Stacia wanted more of everything. More of Walker and the lingering kiss was a start in the right direction. As he let her tongue explore his mouth she learned something about the man in her arms. He wasn't the wall of cold steel she'd thought. There was more to Walker than his hard exterior. She pulled away and dragged her fingers down his shirt, unbuttoning a few buttons as she went.

Walker's gaze moved over her shoulder and his body stiffened. "What is it, Benjamin?"

Stacia turned. Benjamin's eyes held a pained stare. "What's wrong?" She shook her head slowly as she tried to work a swallow. Benjamin winced, and she knew. She felt it in her bones. "Please tell me this has nothing to do with my father. Tell me!" Her voice rose to a scream as tears fell over her cheeks.

"I'm sorry. Cleveland police found his body last night in his car parked on the side of the road. He was shot," he said in almost a whisper.

"No, no, no. no. That can't be. He was protected. You said he would be protected." She fell into Walker's arms and pounded his chest with her first.

"I'm so sorry, Princess. I'm so, so sorry." Walker wrapped his arms around her and stroked her hair.

"I don't understand. Why was he out? I thought he was supposed to stay in the house."

"He was. I don't know what made him leave or where he was going. We haven't had a report from him in a few days. I sent Potter back to check on him. We'll find out what happened and we'll make Carlo pay." Walker pulled back and met her gaze. "I promise."

A wave of tears rolled from her eyes. "It's my fault." Stacia stepped out of his embrace and hugged her chest, suddenly feeling very much alone.

Walker shook his head. "It's not your fault. It's no one's fault. Your father knew the risk. He died doing exactly what kept him going. The last thing he said to me was to take care of you. I won't rest until Carlo is burning in hell."

Her gaze steadied on Walker through her tears. "*We* won't rest. You need to let me in. No more secrets. I need to be on the inside. I want to be part of Platinum."

Walker nodded and cupped her face in his hand.

"You've earned it and more. We'll do it together. But you have to make me a promise." He swiped his thumb over her cheek.

"What?"

"You'll be safe. I won't lose the woman I love."

She nodded and tipped her face to his. "I love you," she whispered and wrapped her arms around his chest pulling his heat into her flesh, drawing off its strength. Her life had just turned on in axis and flung everything she knew into the wind, never to be seen again. Her world was shattered. All she had left was the man in her arms and the desire to take revenge on the devil himself.

The End

www.sandrabunino.com

EVERNIGHT PUBLISHING ®

www.evernightpublishing.com